California Nurses

Welcome to Leanora Paz Memorial Hospital!

Roommates Serena Dias and Avery Smith
have done it! They are *officially* qualified nurses.
And they're ready to hit the wards of
Leanora Paz Memorial Hospital and save lives!
While it's never easy to start a new job,
Serena and Avery are about to face more obstacles
than most new nurses. Because Serena has a
nine-month secret that she *can't* keep from surgeon
Tobias Renfro. And Avery has a billion dollar secret
that he *must* keep from Dr. Robyn Callaghan!

Escape to San Diego with…

Serena and Toby's Story
The Nurse's One-Night Baby by Tina Beckett

And

Avery and Roby's Story
Nurse with a Billion Dollar Secret by Scarlet Wilson

Available now!

Dear Reader,

There's something so nice about writing a duet with another author. Tina and I started writing medical romances around the same time and it was so nice to brainstorm with her about our apartment-sharing fellow nurses. This is also the first time I've written a male nurse, so that was fun!

Avery and Robyn both have nicknames. He's Mr. Sunshine and she's Dr. Grumpy, but in the San Diego hospital where they are working, opposites clearly attract. One has hidden secrets, and the other has a childhood past that has had a lasting impact on their life. Working these two through these big life issues was challenging in order to bring them to their happy ending.

This book is coming out around International Nurses Day. I've been a nurse in the NHS in Scotland for over thirty years and I don't regret a single second—even in the tough times over the last few years. So I want to wish all nurses, all over the world, happy International Nurses Day—you do a spectacular job!

Best wishes,

Scarlet Wilson

NURSE WITH A BILLION DOLLAR SECRET

SCARLET WILSON

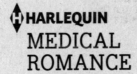

HARLEQUIN

MEDICAL
ROMANCE

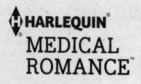

HARLEQUIN®
MEDICAL
ROMANCE™

Recycling programs
for this product may
not exist in your area.

ISBN-13: 978-1-335-73781-6

Nurse with a Billion Dollar Secret

Harlequin Enterprises ULC
22 Adelaide St. West, 41st Floor
Toronto, Ontario M5H 4E3, Canada
www.Harlequin.com

Printed in U.S.A.

Scarlet Wilson wrote her first story aged eight and has never stopped. She's worked in the health service for twenty years, having trained as a nurse and a health visitor. Scarlet now works in public health and lives on the west coast of Scotland with her fiancé and their two sons. Writing medical romances and contemporary romances is a dream come true for her.

Books by Scarlet Wilson

Harlequin Medical Romance

Night Shift in Barcelona
The Night They Never Forgot

Neonatal Nurses
Neonatal Doc on Her Doorstep

The Christmas Project
A Festive Fling in Stockholm

Double Miracle at St. Nicolino's Hospital
Reawakened by the Italian Surgeon

Marriage Miracle in Emergency
Snowed In with the Surgeon

Visit the Author Profile page
at Harlequin.com for more titles.

This book is dedicated to my fellow nurses
all over the world on International Nurses Day.
Thank you for the job that you do.

CHAPTER ONE

THE DAY WASN'T supposed to start out like this. It just wasn't. Dr Robyn Callaghan pushed her hair out of her face for around the twentieth time and wondered why the air-conditioned hospital seemed to be keeping everyone cool but her.

She could feel a horrible trickle down her spine as she climbed the stairs—two at a time—to answer her sixth page of the morning. Her breakfast/lunch was still sitting on the cafeteria table, next to her coffee. There hadn't been time to eat it. She'd need to remind herself about the solitary banana in her pocket whenever she finally got a minute.

She pushed open the doors to the cardiac floor and made it three steps before the arrest page sounded. No. Not again. She didn't even listen to the rest of the message.

She looked up as she heard the echo of a similar page nearby and started running to the coronary care unit. She'd already attended two arrests in the unit that morning.

A large guy barrelled out of the door to her left and almost straight into her. Thankfully, his broad frame was deceiving; this guy could move like a dancer, as he dodged around her and gave her a half-amused smile. 'Wrong way,' he said as the rest of the arrest message was repeated.

'Cardiac arrest. Main door, front entrance.'

Robyn nearly swore out loud. She spun around and darted after Mr Light-on-his-Feet as he disappeared through the door to the stairway. If the page had only gone off three minutes earlier, she would have saved herself a stair climb.

Her heart thudded as she tried to keep up with her athletic colleague. As he reached the ground floor he paused for a moment and held the door open for her.

'Thanks,' she breathed as she ran through and straight along the corridor to the main entrance. She could already see the commotion in front of them. A man in a suit was lying on the ground, a few people on their knees around him.

As she got closer she realised a nurse was already performing CPR on him. 'I'll get the cart,' she said, darting to the right, where the outpatient department was based.

The bright red emergency trolley was fully stocked and sitting directly outside one of the consulting rooms. Robyn grabbed it and ran back to the main entrance, her brain going into automatic pilot. She lifted the defibrillator from the trolley, peeling the labels from the two pads, and positioned herself above the person doing cardiac massage.

The nurse stopped massage for a few seconds, and opened the man's shirt, allowing Robyn to slap the pads onto his chest. It only took the machine a few seconds to read his heart rhythm.

The man from the cardiac unit grabbed a bag and mask from the cart, positioned it appropriately and started to bag air into the guy's lungs. It was clear from his colour he wasn't breathing for himself.

All eyes were fixed on the monitor. Two seconds later it went dead.

Robyn leaned over and gave it a knock. She'd never seen a defib turn itself off. The nurse in pale pink scrubs on the floor seemed stunned. But the guy—the dancer—in the green scrubs of the cardiac unit raised his eyebrows and got to his feet. 'First time for everything. I'll get another.'

He took off at a run, leaving Robyn and the outpatient nurse staring in dismay at each other. A little light flicked in Robyn's brain. If she told her medic friends this at a later date they would all shake their heads in horror. But Robyn refused to let panic anywhere near her. While a defib was now considered an essential part of a hospital's equipment, at some stage they hadn't existed. 'You bag, I'll do massage,' Robyn said to the nurse, hoping to kick-start her natural instincts again.

In an ideal world, she'd be trying to get venous access by inserting a cannula—but right now, that would have to wait. Come to think of it—where was the anaesthetist? There was usually one who responded swiftly to an arrest page, but, no matter how hard she strained her ears, she couldn't hear the sound of any other pairs of running feet.

One of the hospital porters came out of a nearby room, blinked twice, then leaned over. 'Shall I get you guys a trolley?'

They both nodded, Robyn as she started chest compressions, and the nurse, who inserted an airway and started bagging the patient.

'Do you know anything about this man?' Robyn asked the nurse.

She shook her head and gave a half-smile.

'I was just going on my break.' She glanced over her shoulder. The doors to Outpatients were closed behind her. 'They'll think I'm in the canteen.'

'Robyn Callaghan,' Robyn said quickly. 'Just started my cardiac rotation here.'

'Monica Garske,' said the nurse. 'Been in Outpatients for twenty years and never had a cardiac arrest.' She smiled nervously.

A firm hand landed on her shoulder. 'And you're doing a great job.' The guy in the green scrubs dropped to his knees. He had another defib in his hands and swopped the pads over in a virtually seamless motion. He pressed the button on the machine as an older man appeared, slightly sweaty, and stared down at them. The anaesthetist had finally arrived.

'Tell me we can get this guy a little higher. I don't think my back can take it.'

'Don't worry, Joel,' said Mr Green Scrubs smoothly. 'Ardo is on his way with a trolley. I'll get him up for you.'

Robyn's eyes were on the monitor again. 'Ventricular fibrillation,' she said, perfectly in time with her green-scrubs-wearing counterpart. Their eyes locked for a moment and her breath caught somewhere at the back of her throat. He might have been kneeling next to her, but she hadn't really looked at him yet. Not properly.

And now was certainly not the time.

If she had the time, she might consider that the green of his scrubs definitely brought out the green in his eyes. His tanned skin and slightly longer dark hair made him resemble that Italian male model from years ago who had appeared out of water in very tight white trunks, advertising aftershave.

If she'd had the time, she might have lingered on all of that. But the human brain was amazing, and all that flitted through her mind in the literal blink of an eye.

'Charging,' she said, leaning forward, pressing the button and sweeping her gaze around. 'Clear, everyone.'

Hands were lifted and everyone stepped back. The man's body shuddered but the heart rate remained unchanged.

A trolley rolled next to them, and a plastic sliding mat appeared in the corner of her eye. Five seconds. That was all it took to slide the flexible plastic mat under the man and lift him up onto the trolley, the defib being lifted second and placed next to his chest.

'Clear,' Robyn said again, as if this were the most regular thing in the world. In an ideal world, she would have had the time to take him into a suitable room and do a proper assessment. But cardiac arrests were pesky. They didn't give anyone time. In fact, they were the direct enemy of time. And she knew the sooner they could shock him out of this rhythm, the better.

'Clear,' she said as she pressed the button again and electric charge was applied directly to the gelled pads on his chest.

Again, there was no response. She flicked the switch to turn up the joules. As she turned back she saw that the older anaesthetist was checking the patient's airway, and Mr Green Scrubs was tapping his arm, ready to slide a cannula in place to give them venous access. She might not know either of these individuals yet, but everyone clearly knew their job.

She waited the few seconds it took for the cannula to slide into the vein and be secured and tried not to be put out. Sometimes siting a cannula was a pain in the neck. Lots of patients had tricky veins, small and delicate, that would collapse as soon as anyone tried to get access. But her colleague had slid it into place as if it were the easiest thing in the world.

The defib showed it was ready and she checked again. 'Clear,' she announced, giving a nod when everyone had lifted their hands from the patient.

His body arched and after an ominous pause the heart tracing changed, giving a few spread-out beeps. Robyn held her breath. 'Sinus rhythm, bradycardic,' she said.

'ER or Coronary Care?' asked the anaesthetist.

'ER,' said Mr Green Scrubs, just as she said, 'Coronary Care.'

She stared at him, hard. She was the physician leading the crash team. This should be her call.

'No beds in Coronary Care,' he said with an apologetic smile. 'ER for now, and I'll go up and clear a bed for you once we have this man stabilised.'

He was annoying her now. 'And you are?'

There it was again. That tiny quirk of the eyebrow. She was being rude, and she knew it. But he hadn't introduced himself.

'Avery Smith, Coronary Care Unit.' He had a broad smile on his face. And it didn't help. Because this guy was more handsome than was healthy for a work environment.

'Robyn Callaghan, I'm your new doctor,' she said briskly.

A figure appeared next to her, pulling up the side rail and clipping it into place. 'ER it is,' said the porter and started wheeling the trolley.

Avery kept pace, automatically clipping his

side rail into place and talking to the anaesthetist. 'Didn't think you had the page today, Joel.'

'I didn't, but Emmanuel's wife decided to go into early labour. He had to leave.'

Avery's face instantly creased. 'Gemma's okay, though? What is she—three weeks early?'

Joel gave him a knowing smile and nodded. 'You remember everything, and yes. There's no big problem, though. Her waters broke earlier, and she started to labour, so called Emmanuel to tell him she was heading in. I've never seen anyone happier.'

'So why the long face?' asked Avery. 'Did you really not want to carry the page that much?' His voice held a hint of teasing in it.

Joel shook his head. 'No, but it means I've lost the theatre wager on the baby's date of birth.'

Avery let out a laugh as the automatic doors to the ER opened and they rolled the trolley down towards the resus rooms. A harassed-looking woman with messy blonde hair frowned at them. 'What's this?'

Robyn bristled at the woman's tone, about to reply, but Avery got in there first. 'This…' he paused at the word, making a point, but in a much smoother way than she would have '…is a gentleman who had a cardiac arrest at the front door. I haven't managed to get his wallet out yet because we've had to shock him three times to get him back into sinus rhythm. Coronary Care is full, so could you give us some space so our doctor, Robyn—' he said her name as if they were best friends '—can stabilise our man, while I go up and free up a bed for him upstairs?'

The woman rolled her eyes and let out a sigh. 'Fine.' She gestured with her head sideways. 'In there. But don't be long. This place has been hectic all day.' She gave Robyn a stern glance. 'And I can't free you up a nurse.'

This time Robyn couldn't help herself. 'If he'd collapsed in the entrance way of your ER, could you have freed me up a nurse then?'

She could almost see the cogs and wheels of the woman's brain turning. Robyn's Scottish accent always got stronger when she was annoyed, and right now she was distinctly irritated. It took a few seconds for her counterpart to make sense of what she had said.

'Fine.' The woman turned to face Avery. 'But I need my room back in an hour.' She turned and headed out of the door.

'Is everyone here always this friendly?' muttered Robyn under her breath as her patient groaned. She moved forward and talked slowly. 'Hi there, I'm Robyn. You're at Leonora Paz

Memorial Hospital. I'm one of the doctors. Do you remember anything at all?'

The man took a few moments, then shook his head, confusion all over his face. Avery moved into full charm mode on the other side of him. 'I'm Avery, one of the nursing staff. You're in the ER. Can I just check inside your jacket pocket? We want to get your name and details.'

The man gave a brief nod, and Avery slid his hand inside, pulling out a wallet he flipped open. 'Hal Delaney?'

The man gave another nod, and Avery turned the driver's licence to a colleague behind him to take some details. 'Can I let someone know you are here?'

Hal sighed, clearly still confused, and patted his trouser pockets. After a few seconds, he realised his shirt was wide open and there were pads on his chest. 'What happened…?' he asked.

Robyn wasn't happy. She wanted to look after her patient properly, and the noisy ER wasn't ideal. She gently peeled the defib pads from Hal's chest and put on some electrodes from a nearby cardiac monitor, fastening a blood-pressure cuff to his arm.

'Hal,' she said in a low voice. 'We need to have a chat. Your heart wasn't beating properly.

You collapsed in the entrance way of the hospital. We had to give you some electric shocks.'

Hal's eyes widened. He looked terrified.

She kept her voice steady. 'Did you come here to visit someone? Or did you come to the hospital because you weren't feeling well?'

He shook his head. 'No,' he said. 'I had an appointment.'

'At Outpatients?' asked Robyn.

Hal shook his head again. 'With Mr Paz.'

It was only for a split second, but Robyn noticed it. Avery froze. It was as if he'd been caught in a set of headlights.

Robyn was new here. But she knew the hospital had been built as a memorial to the wife of a wealthy billionaire businessman, who had died years earlier. The Paz surname was apparently synonymous with wealth beyond measure in the San Diego area. She was sure that the Mr Paz he was meeting wasn't the original Mr Paz, but maybe it was his son, or grandson?

She pretended not to notice Avery's frozen position and turned to the nursing assistant behind her. 'Can you dial up to the office of Mr Paz and let the secretary know that Mr Delaney has taken unwell, and is currently in the ER?'

The nursing assistant beamed, delighted to have such an important job. Avery, on the other hand, was doing his best to look composed.

'I'll go and clear a bed for you upstairs,' he said smoothly. 'I'll phone down when it's free and we can arrange to transfer Mr Delaney upstairs.'

Robyn wanted to pay more attention to her brand-new colleague's hasty departure. But her head was full of ECG tracings, ordering blood tests, a possible chest X-ray, and administering some medicines to Mr Delaney. Whatever was going on with Avery would have to wait.

'Fine,' she murmured, averting her gaze back to dealing with her patient as Avery hurried off down the corridor. She ordered some tests, and sat down next to Hal, ready to take his history. Her stomach growled loudly, and she remembered the breakfast/lunch still at the cafeteria that she'd never get back to.

Hal was starting to get a little more colour in his cheeks now. He pressed a hand to his chest. 'Ouch,' he said. 'It's sore.'

Robyn nodded. 'Chest compressions. Don't worry—we'll check to make sure you have no broken ribs. You managed to catch everyone's attention today.' She clocked the blood-pressure reading on the monitor. It was surprisingly low.

'Have you been feeling unwell at all?'

She ran through the usual questions quickly, trying to build a picture as to why Hal had collapsed today inside the hospital entrance.

Before she had a chance to complete her history-taking, a tall, broad-shouldered man appeared in the doorway, obviously not waiting for any kind of permission to enter. 'Hal, how are you?'

Robyn was a little taken aback. She stood swiftly. 'I'm afraid Mr Delaney isn't fit for visitors right now.'

It was as if she hadn't spoken at all. The man ignored her and walked around to clasp Hal's hand in both of his. 'This is a fine way to get out of a business meeting.'

'I'm sorry,' said Robyn quickly. 'But I'm in the middle of a consultation. You'll have to wait outside.'

The ER manager appeared in the doorway looking instantly flustered. He was usually as cool as a cucumber, but today was practically flapping.

He gave Robyn a quick anxious glance. She could tell he wasn't delighted that she was the doctor in the resus room.

'Jon,' she said stiffly, 'I've just resuscitated Mr Delaney at the front door. I need time to assess and treat him. Could you escort this visitor out, so I can take care of my patient?'

There was an uneasy silence. A long, long silence.

Jon gave a nervous laugh. 'Robyn, Dr Callaghan, let me introduce you to Mr Paz, our hospital chief executive.'

Robyn blinked. She nodded. 'Pleased to meet you. I'm sure you understand that, right now, it's essential I provide the best care to your friend. In order to do that, I need to take a full history, order some more tests and do a full assessment.'

She could swear Jon had just turned five shades paler than white. Mr Paz was clearly the main man around here. But she was a doctor. Should she just stop treating a patient to let a business friend interrupt what could be critical care? As the thought formed in her brain, her body moved automatically to get between Mr Paz and her patient. 'Why don't you let me call you back when I'm finished? As soon as our tests are completed and Mr Delaney is stable, we will be moving him up to the coronary care unit. I'm sure you can visit him there.'

There was a not so friendly smile on her face, and every muscle in her body was tensed.

It wasn't that Robyn didn't like rich people. It was just their sense of entitlement she didn't like. Growing up in a poverty-stricken part of Glasgow, Robyn had been luckier than most. She'd done well at school and had interviewed successfully enough to get a place at medical school. While the fees were covered, the food, lodgings and placements at hospitals around Scotland weren't. Some grants had helped, along with the biggest variety of part-time jobs. She'd delivered pizzas, worked in a nursing home, a supermarket, a library, a gym, and a bar.

She'd trained alongside some others from rich families. While she'd worked back-breaking hours over and above her studies and placements just to survive, they'd swanned around in their flash cars, showed off their apartments and all their latest technology. Robyn could have lived with all that.

What she hadn't liked—or stood for—was some of the entitled attitudes the rich had towards those less fortunate than themselves. It made her blood boil. So, any time she was around someone who was clearly richer than King Midas, it made her twitchy.

It hadn't helped that the one time she'd risked dating someone in the richer-than-rich category, it hadn't taken all that long to realise he wasn't with her because he actually wanted to have a relationship with her. He was there because she was smarter than him and could help him with his studies. Finding out he'd only been amusing himself with her, until he could find a wealthier replacement with better connections, who could help him with his longer-term career prospects, had been a bitter sting. It had made her resentment against inherited wealth and the entitlement of the richer classes, and her strong desire to work herself out of poverty, even stronger.

There was a good thing about being a stubborn Scots girl. She didn't feel obliged to fill the silence. She just let her words sit with Mr Paz. Robyn was also a master at staring out people. She'd learned that in her days as a steward at the football stadium for one of the two rival teams in Glasgow, when she'd had to deal with sometimes drunk, troublesome fans. It had stood her in good stead.

Jon coughed. It suddenly struck her that she might not be doing herself any favours. She was new here. She'd only met the head of the ER briefly in passing. She'd certainly never met the chief executive of the hospital.

'Mr Paz, shall we give Dr Callaghan some time to finish with your friend?' Jon suggested, breaking the standoff.

Mr Paz gave his friend's hand another squeeze. 'I'll see you upstairs, Hal, and I'll make sure our top cardiac physician takes care of you.' He gave Robyn a hard stare and left the room. Jon moved to follow but Robyn switched on a bright smile.

'Can you spare me a nurse? I've got a few

things still to complete, and it will go quicker if I have someone familiar with everything.'

Jon looked as if he wanted to say a whole lot more, but his gaze fixed on Mr Paz's retreating back and he flinched. 'Fine,' he muttered as he walked out of the door.

Five hours later Robyn was knackered. She'd accompanied Hal up in the elevator, helped him transfer into the coronary care bed, given a rundown to his assigned nurse, and talked over the tests, results and findings with the stern-faced senior physician.

She'd done a good job. She always did. But she couldn't help wondering if she'd just done herself no favours in her new work environment.

By the time she headed out to the nursing station she could have easily sat in a chair and cried. That, or mugged someone for any single snippet of food they might have on their person.

She finished inputting some final details into a chart and looked around. Nurses' stations were usually a mecca for food. But this station was pristine. Not the usual ramshackle collection of half-chewed pens left by drug reps, or scraps of paper with indistinguishable notes. Not even a half-opened packet of biscuits. This was the poorest excuse for a nurses' station she'd ever visited.

Robyn sighed and walked towards the treatment room. She could hear the murmur of voices. 'We've got Dr Grumpy covering for us for the next six months.'

'Which one is Dr Grumpy?'

'The girl with red hair. She's Scottish. Pale skinned. I suppose she's pretty enough.'

Robyn stopped walking.

'So how did she earn the nickname of Dr Grumpy already? She hasn't been here long.'

'My friend works in the cath lab. She was apparently quite nervous when she started. Bumped a tray in the cath lab when observing an angiogram and put the whole procedure back. Apparently she's been walking about scowling ever since.'

'Who was doing the angio?'

'Raul Hempur.'

'Dracula? Oh, no. Making a mistake around him would be my worst nightmare.'

'Well, apparently it was hers.'

There was some laughter and a rustle of something that sounded suspiciously like a packet of sweets. Robyn had started to take a few backward steps, deciding it was definitely time to retreat, but just as she lifted her head Avery Smith came walking out of a patient's room.

This time it was Robyn's turn to freeze and cringe all at once.

This cannot be happening.

'Dr Callaghan? Everything okay?'

Humiliation for Beginners was not a class she intended attending today. She shook her head and strode forward into the treatment room and looked the three staff in the eye. 'Dr Grumpy at your service! I don't suppose you've got any food around here? Cafeteria's closed and I'm afraid I'm absolutely starving. I haven't eaten today yet.'

There it was again. The three brains having to process what she'd said, because she was annoyed so was speaking quicker, with a strong accent. This was going to get old very quickly.

She could sense Avery's presence at her back. Three sets of eyes were squirming in front of her as they finally deciphered what she'd said. One was a nurse, one a physio and one a cardiac tech. It was the tech that handed over a half-empty packet of sweets, with an apologetic shrug. 'Here you go.'

'Thanks. And it's Robyn, by the way.'

A light hand touched her shoulder. 'Why don't I show you where the staffroom is? You can have a seat for five minutes and take a break.'

She bristled, about to tell Avery Smith she didn't need a break. She knew he was trying to be a peacekeeper. But he added, 'We have a coffee machine,' and the magic words made her instantly more pliable.

She didn't look back at the other three staff, just made her way out of the door. 'I hope it's good coffee,' she said. He nodded and led her further down the corridor and into a medium-sized room with a small table and chairs, some cupboards, a sink, microwave, comfortable chairs and, yes, a coffee machine, which was bubbling and sending off delicious aromas in her direction.

Robyn didn't wait to be shown what to do. She'd been first a medical student, and then a doctor too long. She moved over, opened a cupboard to grab a mug, and poured herself some coffee from the jug. She reached into her pocket for some artificial sweetener, popped two in and stood back for a moment with the mug in her hands, just letting the smell drift around her. She closed her eyes and breathed.

She was aware of the silence and eventually opened her eyes again. Avery Smith was staring straight at her with an amused expression on his face. Now she was finally getting a chance to get a better look at this guy. If he could stare at her, she could stare at him.

He definitely looked like the brother of the aftershave model. His scrubs showcased his broad shoulders, sculpted chest and long limbs. But the clear green eyes were his most distinguishable feature. They were still staring at her.

'Sorry, was I supposed to pour you a cup too?'

He laughed and shook his head, ignoring her slightly sarcastic remark, and got himself a cup, pouring coffee and then reaching down into a refrigerator next to the sink. She'd missed that. He smelled the milk, checked the date, before pouring it into his mug. 'Milk?' he asked.

She couldn't help but finally smile. 'The familiar actions of someone who's worked in a hospital too long.' She held out her mug for him to add a splash of milk.

He tapped a sign on the front of the refrigerator. 'Some desperate soul actually put a note up here, trying to get people to put the freshest milk at the back of the fridge to make sure things rotated.'

Now Robyn laughed. 'Fool. Did they actually expect that to work?'

She reached into the packet of sweets—it was actually chocolate-covered biscuits, but they would do—and pulled out two before flopping onto one of the old comfy chairs.

She took a sip of her coffee, a bite of one of the biscuits as her stomach grumbled loudly. Avery laughed as heat rushed into her cheeks.

She owned it, and patted her stomach. 'Haven't eaten properly since last night. I did buy food in the cafeteria earlier, but the arrest page went off before I had a chance to eat it.'

He gave her a curious look. 'How many times has that page gone today?'

She raised her eyebrows. 'Don't you know the rules? We don't talk about fight club.'

His smile broadened at her movie joke. In Robyn's experience, as soon as you talked about the arrest page, you cursed yourself, and it would usually go off in the next few minutes.

'I'll give you that one,' he agreed.

She took another bite of the biscuit. 'Six is the answer.'

'That many?' He sat forward. 'I took the page when I came on duty this morning. The arrest at the main door was my first.'

She frowned. 'I thought the nursing staff started at six?'

He sighed. 'We do. It's officially my day off. I'm supposed to be working at the free clinic in the heart of the city, but someone here called in sick.' He leaned back again. 'Or maybe they went home sick after so many calls.' He held up his hands. 'Who knows? I didn't really have time to ask. I'd just come on duty, saw the unit was full, and took the page before it went off.'

He settled back into the chair a bit more. 'And don't mind what the others were saying back there. They give everyone nicknames.'

'Really? What's yours?'

He shifted, his comfortable chair obviously becoming uncomfortable—then pulled a face. 'Mr Sunshine,' he admitted.

She groaned and closed her eyes. 'You have got to be kidding me! So, you're Mr Sunshine, and I'm Dr Grumpy? No way.'

He waved his hand. 'You've just got here. They don't know you yet.'

She raised one eyebrow. 'Well, just wait until they know me. My nickname will be ten times worse than Dr Grumpy.' She wrinkled her nose. 'And who will cover your shift at the free clinic if you're here?'

He sipped his coffee. 'I swapped it with a friend. I'll work this Sunday instead. I wouldn't let them down. Now, tell me a bit about yourself. I love your accent.'

Robyn tried not to avert her gaze. She hated personal questions and tried to give away as little as possible about herself. 'You first,' she challenged.

He licked his lips for a second, then nodded. 'Well, I'm Avery Smith, I'm twenty-six. Trained as nurse. Born and brought up in San Diego. Chose to work in the cardiac unit because I just love everything about the science. I love the transplant work, the surgeries, the implantable defibs, the pacing wires, the management of the heart failure patients, the angiograms, the MI work.' He waved his hand. 'I could go on and on.'

She gave a small smile. 'So, it's where your heart is?'

'Exactly.' He grinned at her very poor joke. 'If you do a surgical rotation, you might meet my best friend. Serena Dias works in Critical Care. We did our training together and shared an apartment for a while.' He gave a mild shake of his head. 'That was before, of course, she met the love of her life, Toby Renfro. He's one of the surgeons here, and they've just moved in together.'

'So, you've been left high and dry?' Robyn quipped.

He shrugged. 'You could say that.' He leaned forward, putting his elbows on his knees. 'Or you could say that I'm delighted that my best friend has found her happy ever after. She deserves it.'

'Sunshine by name, sunshine by nature? Do you ever get grumpy?'

He finished his coffee. 'I try not to. Life's too short. Now, don't think you're getting away with not telling me more about yourself. Play fair.'

Robyn forced a smile. 'So, I did my medical training in Glasgow, I was born and brought up there. Did my first year in a hospital in Aberdeen, then joined a new programme where you traded places with someone from another country, in an already established programme there.' She held up her hands. 'I ended up here.'

'You didn't choose here?' Avery seemed surprised.

'You only get to choose the country, not the actual hospital. I did a placement in Germany first, and this time in the US.'

She tried to work out the expression on his face. 'Most doctors or trainees who come here have gone through rigorous selection procedures. Paz Memorial is renowned for its cardiology department, its surgeons and its techniques. Some people try for years to get a job here,' he said.

The implication was clear. He didn't approve of her. She wasn't good enough. He might be Mr Sunshine for the rest of the world. But he didn't look remotely sunny from where Robyn was sitting.

'Like you?' she said, letting the sarcasm drip from her tone.

It was almost as if he'd switched off, being so focused on how elite this hospital was. 'Only a few from my nursing class were successful in getting jobs here.'

'Did you have to go through a rigorous selection process?' She was getting angry now. Was he doing this deliberately?

'Four interviews,' he said without hesitation.

She leaned forward, into a similar position as he'd adopted. 'And what makes you think for a second that I didn't?'

He blinked. She let him process that for a few seconds.

'The international programme had seventy thousand worldwide applicants. They picked one hundred.' She stood up. 'Sadly, I wasn't their number one pick, but I was the number two.' She watched his eyes widen at her statement. 'So, I more than earned my place here. But don't try and talk to me about selection processes. I've spent my life seeing how unfair some selection processes can be—unless, of course, you have a large bank balance.'

He blanched, then quickly stood up too. 'What's that supposed to mean?'

'I mean that often those from the wealthiest families get the best placements, or the settings that they want. It was certainly like that for me when I was back in medical school. The selection process for this programme was the first time I felt as if things were fundamentally fair. I actually had a fighting chance to be picked because of my scores and not my bank balance.'

Avery was looking at her with a deep frown in his forehead, as if he didn't quite know what to say to that.

The door opened and another nurse walked in, took one look at them both, turned on her heel and walked back out.

Robyn felt exasperated. She waved her hand. 'Might as well earn my new nickname.'

She watched as Avery took a few long, calming breaths, wondering what on earth she'd said that had set him off. He raised his eyes to hers. 'I think we got off on the wrong foot.' He put his hand on his chest. 'I love this place. I'm passionate about it. Paz Memorial has a great reputation and it matters to me—' he shook his head '—for reasons I can't really explain. I didn't know about your programme. Most doctors have to apply or specially request to continue their training here. Competition is tough.' He hesitated for a second, 'And I'm sure bank balance doesn't matter in the selection process. But I'm sorry, I didn't mean to sound defensive.'

'I think we did get off on the wrong foot,' replied Robyn quickly, turning his explanation over in her head. What reasons could he not explain? 'But then, you did abandon me down in the ER earlier.' She put her hands on her hips.

'I did not.'

'Oh, own it, Avery. As soon as that hospital CEO appeared, you practically broke the record for the four-minute mile. What was that all about?'

She saw something flash across his eyes. Anger? Annoyance? Fear? She couldn't quite put her finger on it.

'I did not,' he said defensively. 'I'd just started work and already knew the unit had no free space. The most useful thing I could do for you was to come up here and clear a bed for you, so Mr Delaney could get the expert care that he needs.'

'Sounds like you read that straight from the brochure,' she said sarcastically.

He shook his head.

'So, you really think the best thing you can do, the first time you meet a new doctor, carrying the arrest page, is to leave her in an unfamiliar environment, with staff she doesn't know, and procedures she's not used to?'

She saw his jaw clench. 'I might not have met you before, but I had no idea you'd never been inside the ER before. I'm not responsible for the induction of new staff. That should have been covered before you started. You should know all the procedures by now and you were with the head of the ER; you couldn't have been in better hands.'

Robyn hadn't moved her hands from her hips. Six months. That was how long she was going to be here. She wanted to learn everything that she could from all members of the team. Why did she have to get stuck with this guy? He was clearly a fake. Everyone else called him Mr Sunshine. But she wasn't fooled for a second.

Her back ached. She hadn't slept the last two nights because the room the hospital had given her backed onto the kitchens, where deliveries seemed to come all hours of the night. She was tired. She was still hungry. And some of the staff here were already talking about her snidely.

Robyn might excel at all things medical, but she readily admitted that her people skills were always a little trickier to negotiate.

She sighed. 'From my perspective, you practically raced out of the ER. You weren't even sure our patient was stable enough to leave. One thing you will learn about me, Avery, is that I call things the way I see them.'

He frowned and held out his arm. 'Did I clear a bed for you?'

She gritted her teeth but nodded.

'And is the cardiac unit the best place for Mr Delaney right now?'

She nodded again.

'Then, things have happened the way they should. You're imagining things. Maybe you're tired. Maybe you need to sit down, take a break, and get a proper meal. It's overwhelming coming to a new place. And as for the procedures, I can take some time to go over them with you if you want. All the staff here are willing to help our new doctors. All you have to do is ask.'

'It's hard to ask when they're too busy gossiping and name-calling.'

Avery drew in a deep breath, gave a conciliatory nod and lifted his left hand. 'You're right. I'm sorry about that. I'll talk to them. That's not the kind of unit that we run.'

He was being nice now. But it wasn't helping.

'I'm a big girl,' she said as she raised her chin. 'I don't need your pity.'

She turned and headed to the door, her stomach growling again. Her footsteps slowed and she reached back and picked up what was left of the chocolate biscuits, aware that his green eyes were still on her.

She gave a toss of her hair and walked out of the room, glancing at her watch and heading to the nurses' station. She was due off duty and she couldn't wait to hand over this page and get out of here.

Maybe coming to San Diego hadn't been such a good idea after all.

CHAPTER TWO

'You did what?' Serena threw back her head and laughed.

Avery groaned as he sipped his coffee. 'Stop, you're not helping. I can't remember ever making such a bad impression on someone before.'

'No, you're just used to charming your way around this place with a big grin on your face. She might have the nickname of grumpy, but maybe she's just the one girl that will make you work harder to prove yourself.'

He set down his spoon and stared at his friend. 'Why would you say something like that?'

Serena started dissecting the plum and apple she'd bought in the cafeteria. They were sitting outside the main eating area in the central courtyard—usually a suntrap, but today was warm but cloudy. It was away from the throng of the main cafeteria and offered a little more privacy, with tables and benches, a winding path, and plenty of greenery around.

She grinned at him. She hadn't even answered yet and he was already shaking his head. 'You're in that crazy-in-love stage. You want to imagine pairing up everyone round about you into couples and happy families. Believe me, our Scots girl is more likely to chase me with an axe than anything else.'

Serena leaned her head in one hand and looked a bit dreamy. 'There's nothing wrong with a bit of happiness.'

He gave a conciliatory nod. They'd shared an apartment for over three years. He knew Serena better than anyone, and he'd never seen her so happy since she'd got together with Toby.

'Guess what happened now you've moved out?'

'What?'

'The dishwasher broke. I swear it always worked perfectly for you, and never for me. Now that it knows you're gone—it's decided to go on strike.'

She laughed. 'You just don't talk nice to it, that's what's wrong.' Serena gave a wicked grin. 'But then it seems like you don't talk nice to other people too.'

Avery groaned and put his head in his hands. 'I tried my best.' He took a deep breath. 'It didn't help that the patient we'd resuscitated had a special visitor in the ER.'

Serena took a bite of her plum. 'Oh, who?'

'Leo Paz.'

She stopped chewing, her eyes widening. 'No.'

'Yes.'

'Did your uncle recognise you?'

'He didn't get a chance. I was out of there in a flash—another reason Robyn was sore at me. She accused me of abandoning her.'

'Well, did you?'

Avery cringed and looked upwards. 'No, yes, maybe....'

'Mr Paz.' Serena shook her head. 'I have never seen him the whole time I've been here.'

'Neither have I. Or, at least, I hadn't.'

Serena gave him a curious look. 'What do you think he would have said to you if he had recognised you?'

Avery actually felt sick. 'I don't know. There was such bad blood between him and my mother. If she were still alive, I definitely wouldn't be working here. She would have hated it.'

'I'm not sure she would. Your mother had a good relationship with your grandparents. It's only her siblings that caused trouble.'

Avery smiled. 'Well, she did go out and fall

pregnant to a married man. Scandalous behaviour. My uncle told her that every time he saw her.'

'But, at the end of the day, it was none of his business. You always said your grandparents never said a bad word about your father. It was just a shame that he died when you were so young.'

Avery sighed. 'Money and families complicate everything.' He held up his hands. 'Part of this place is mine since my mother died. But I keep myself hidden for a reason. The rest of the family know I exist, but they have no idea I'm still in San Diego, or that I'm a nurse.'

Serena put her hand over Avery's. 'But your mom had such good care at this hospital. Doesn't working here ever stir up memories for you?'

He looked off into the distance. 'Yes, and no. I'm never in the cancer unit, and her sudden onset leukaemia came on so quickly.' He sighed. 'There are still some things we can't cure. And we all have to live with that. But working here—for me—it helps me honour the memory of my grandparents and mother. My uncle didn't take over as CEO until after my mother died, and I was still young then. I always guessed he just bullied his way into it, like he did with other things in life. Changing my name and keeping away from my uncles and aunts was done at my attorney's advice. He didn't want me to work here. He thought it was too risky. But the last time my uncle saw me I was a young teenager. He certainly wasn't around when my mother got sick, and she was furious at the way her brother steamrollered the rest of the family over the running of the hospital. She didn't want me to have to deal with any of that. She wanted me to be free of all the family drama.'

Serena bit her lip. 'But you trained as a nurse for a reason. You love cardiology. It's natural you want to work in the place that's renowned the world over.' She took a drink from her water bottle. 'It's not your fault this place is named after your grandmother. Maybe if your grandfather was still alive, things would be different.'

He rolled his eyes. 'If my grandfather was still alive, he would be over a hundred.'

Serena gave a soft smile. 'We've had hundred-year-old patients before.' She reached her hand over and squeezed Avery's. 'You've always known that at some point your colleagues might find out your name is Paz and not Smith. There's still a chance you will run into your uncle and he'll recognise you. You need to have a contingency plan in place.'

He finished his coffee. 'Well, I guess I've just ruled running away to Scotland out of the equation. What about France? Or Hawaii? I've always wanted to work there.'

'Are you purposely picking places I'll need to fly to with a baby if I want to visit?'

'You'll be visiting me?

'*We'll* be visiting you. Me, baby and Toby. Stop trying to get away from us. You will still be required to be our babysitter on occasion. No matter where you try to go to.'

Avery squeezed her hand back. 'And I'll be honoured. But in the first instance, I need to try and make up with my department's new doctor.'

Serena frowned. 'Just how grumpy is she?'

He held his hand out and wiggled it. 'I'm not sure. Is she even grumpy? Or is she just bolshie? If what she told me about her selection process is true, then she must be a very good doctor. I think she might just be a straight talker.' He ran his fingers through his dark hair. 'My trouble is, when she starts talking quickly, I struggle to catch everything she says—her accent is really strong—and somehow I know that's not going to help matters.'

'Well, you know how to solve that one, don't you?'

He shook his head, leaning over, grabbing her apple and taking a bite. 'No, how?'

'Hoi.' She slapped his hand away from her apple. 'Stay away from a pregnant woman's food. You're taking your life into your hands here.' She fixed him with a hard stare. 'We're talking about this new doctor quite a lot. What does she look like?'

'What does that have to do with anything?'

'Interesting,' said Serena, looking amused. 'Instantly defensive. Now, tell me what she looks like.'

He made a throwaway gesture with his hand. 'Red hair, but more the brown kind than the ginger kind. Blue eyes. About the same size as yourself.' He rolled his eyes. 'Without the pregnant stomach.' Then he looked thoughtful. 'Or maybe she does have one. But if she does—it's not obvious.'

Serena tilted her head. 'That's a lot of detail. You noticed her eye colour? I'm impressed. And the particular shade of red her hair is? What's happened to you?'

Avery was indignant. 'I'm a nurse. I'm meant to be observant. Have you forgotten that?'

The smile that spread across Serena's face made him want to rapidly change the subject. He knew she would spend the rest of the time teasing him. She tapped her fingers on the table. 'I think it's something else.' Her words had that kind of sing-song tone and he groaned and held up his hand.

'Stop. Let's go back. How do I solve the problem with the accent?'

'Oh, that's easy. The way to get used to her accent is to be around her more. It's simple. You'll get used to it. Just make sure that you spend as much time with her as possible. Oh, and *don't* make her mad.'

'Oh, I don't intend to. Remember that phrase—what was it? *You wouldn't like me when I'm angry.* Said by everybody's favourite green superhero. I think that might apply to her too.'

'You're tough on her,' said Serena with interest. 'Does Mr Sunshine want to spread some of his bright light?'

Avery shook his head at his nickname. 'I can't help the fact I'm a happy individual,' he said. 'My mother says I was born smiling.'

Serena put her hand on her small stomach. 'Well, feel free to spread the sunshine to this one. I would love a happy baby.'

They sat in comfortable silence for a few moments, Avery's mind going back to the recent events with Robyn.

After a few minutes he leaned back from the table, stretching out his back and arms. They were aching. The hospital seemed to be going through a spell of cardiac arrests. Dealing with prolonged arrests was tiring for all involved. 'Six,' he murmured.

'Six what?'

'Arrest calls. That's how many Robyn dealt with on her first shift.'

'No way. What on earth was happening?'

'I don't know.'

'Well, surely that would make anyone grumpy?' Serena looked quite indignant.

'Why do I get the feeling you're going to be *#TeamRobyn*?'

'Because I'm just naturally *#TeamGirl*. But imagine having a day like that, getting deserted in the ER, then going upstairs and hearing the petty nickname you've been given. If it had been me, I would have been wearing the Dr Grumpy nickname with pride.'

Avery let out a slow breath. 'I get it. Plus, it's a new city, a new hospital.' He leaned his head on his hand. 'And I really didn't help things. I was on edge when I saw my uncle and then I think I might have misinterpreted something that she said, and that made me even more defensive.'

Serena took a breath. 'I meant what I said about you needing a contingency plan for if the truth comes out. Particularly if there's a chance you might run into your uncle again.'

Avery sighed. 'I know it. I'm an adult, not a young teenager any more. And I have a stake here—financial and emotional—in this place that I love.' He looked around the courtyard. 'I just don't know if I'm ready to reveal myself. Ready to step up to being a Paz.'

Serena pressed her hand into his shoulder. 'Well, I can't tell you how to deal with your family. But I can give you a hint about Robyn.'

'Go on, then.'

'You need to buy her dessert. Cake. Chocolate. Candies. What do they eat in Scotland?'

'I don't know.'

Serena stood up. 'Well, find out. It's time to start making amends with Dr Grumpy.'

Robyn had spent the last hour trying not to cry. She wouldn't. She just wouldn't. But every time the noisy delivery trucks broke her sleep again, her mind drifted back to a few days ago and the staff in the cardiac unit gossiping about her. As for the disagreement with Avery Smith, her brain wouldn't even let her go there.

She'd messaged her friend, Genevieve, who was working back in Scotland. Ginny always had her back—no matter what else was going on—and Robyn was grateful for the support.

Her placement in Germany had been easier than this. At least she could sleep there. The hospital had put everyone up in studio flats, a five-minute walk from the hospital. All the other doctors had started on the same day as her, and there was a certain camaraderie when everyone learned at the same time.

Here—she'd started a few weeks later than the others due to a mix-up with her working visa. It had been an admin error by the hospital, and Robyn wasn't penalised for it. But it meant the others had already made friends, scored the best rooms, and found their way around the city.

As the beep-beep of yet another van backing up started to sound, she finally gave up on sleep and flung the pillow she'd had over her head away. Nothing could deaden the noise around her. She wasn't even supposed to be working until later.

She showered and grabbed some clothes, tying her long hair up. She had no idea where she was going, but maybe if she went for a jog she could familiarise herself with the city and grab some breakfast.

Paz Memorial wasn't quite on the waterfront of the bay, but it was close enough for Robyn to see the naval boats and head in that direction. It wasn't even six a.m., but she could see a number of early-morning joggers running along the edge of the marina. The paved path was broad and the morning was light and bright. Robyn took it easy, only covering a couple of kilometres before changing direction to run through some of the streets. The Gaslamp district was nearby and Robyn was relieved to see some of the stores were already open. It didn't take her long to inhale the scents of a bakery and join the short line outside. After the last few days she didn't hesitate in ordering two of the wonderful-smelling coffees and three of the mini pastries.

By the time she finished the five-minute walk back to the hospital, one of the coffees was finished, and the three mini pastries were gone. Like all hospitals, Paz Memorial was never quiet. As she walked back through the glass-fronted lobby there were a number of staff all arriving for their shifts. She didn't recognise any of them.

Her heart gave a little pang. This was a big place. With over six hundred beds, and designated Level Two trauma centre for the area. She knew there would be a myriad people working here, would she even have time to make friends?

She paused for a moment, watching the world go by. Her room was too small to spread out comfortably. She'd shower again and head for the library. There were plenty of procedures and protocols she could study before reporting for duty. She might even take a look at some of the listings for apartments nearby. The hospital admin staff were usually good at pointing new staff in the right direction—steering them away from any undesirable areas, or places where transport could be an issue.

Feeling a little more heartened, she turned around and took a step—just as someone collided with her. Her coffee shot up into the air, then down all around her. Robyn let out a gasp as the other person dropped a large white box on the floor with an ominous splat.

'Sorry,' she breathed quickly as the now not so hot coffee dripped from her running gear.

A mild expletive came from the person next to her. Avery Smith had been wearing a white shirt and blue jeans. She doubted that shirt would ever be white again.

Not only had he been doused in coffee, he also had an interesting array of bright red, brown and pink splotches decorating his shirt. She tilted her head. 'What on earth were you carrying?' she asked.

'Dessert,' he said glumly as he picked up the barely together white box and lifted the lid.

Robyn peered inside. 'Yikes.' The jam doughnuts had exploded, and the apple pie had merged into the chocolate cake. 'Is it some-one's birthday?'

He shook his head. 'I was just bringing in some cakes.' He hesitated for a brief second. 'I do that sometimes.'

There was something about the way he said it that was off. She didn't doubt he sometimes brought in cakes for his colleagues, but for some reason she didn't quite believe him.

He held up the box again. 'How about we find some cutlery and just eat what's left?'

Robyn shook her head. 'No. Not for me, thanks. I just had breakfast and am heading to the library before I'm on duty.' She pulled a face. 'Sorry about your clothes.'

Avery shook his head. 'It's fine. I need to put on a uniform anyway.' He gave a small smile at the mangled box. 'See you in the unit later.' There was something resigned about his tone. Was he sorry she was working today? Maybe he didn't want to work with her at all.

Robyn felt instantly defensive. Every part of her prickly. She couldn't find any other words, so she just turned and walked away.

Just over an hour later, Avery was still trying to find a way to make amends with Robyn. In theory, she should also now be trying to make amends with him, but somehow he knew her brain didn't work that way. The doughnuts had been a bust. He couldn't even admit he'd been bringing them in for her as way of an apology—it had just seemed stupid at the time. So now he was back to square one.

He'd walked through the whole unit twice. The cardiac beds, the day beds, the intensive cardiac care unit, the angiograph unit, and the cardiac rehab dept. Robyn was nowhere.

'Anyone know where our new doc is?' he asked a few of the staff at the nurses' station.

'Dr Grumpy?' asked one of the physios.

'Dr Callaghan,' Avery said pointedly.

But this point was lost on the physio. 'She's down in the ER seeing a teenager with potential cardiac issues. I don't think the paediatrician wanted to admit him, but she's having none of it. Last I heard she was trying to page Dr Anker to back her up.'

'Dr Anker?' Avery's eyebrows shot upwards. He let out a groan. Everyone knew that he was the most difficult of their consultants. 'Why would she pick him?'

'Because she has a penchant for tragedy?' suggested the physio, with a shrug.

Of course, he went down to the ER. He didn't even pretend it was for any other reason than to help out their new doctor. One person nodded in solidarity, but another rolled their eyes.

The ER was strangely chaotic for the middle of the week. He saw a nurse colleague and went up alongside him. 'Michael, is there a party and you didn't tell me?'

Michael was loading supplies into his own arms. He turned and automatically loaded some into Avery's. 'We've got a pile-up on the freeway plus a nursing home with norovirus. A medical doctor and an ER doctor off sick, and referrals backed way up. You here to help?'

'I was here to find my new doctor.' He started walking alongside Michael, to wher-ever the supplies were needed. 'But I can call upstairs and tell them you need some help for an hour.'

Michael nodded. 'Great. Your girl is in cu-bicle seven with a kid. Her and the paediatri-cian have fallen out.' He gave Avery a sideways glance. 'I like her. She's smart. She's also of-fered to see a few patients for us. Didn't hes-itate to throw her hat into the ring. Not like other disciplines I can mention.' He scowled at one of the surgical doctors who was practi-cally sprinting out of the department.

He ducked behind some curtains, dumped his supplies and motioned to Avery to put his on a nearby trolley. 'Help is appreciated. Go to the whiteboard and take anything that seems reasonable to you. Shout if you need help.'

Avery swallowed. He was always happy to help, but was aware of his own limitations. He was relatively newly qualified. Most people who worked down in the pit—as they called the ER—had a few years under their belt. But Avery knew he could see a few patients. The elderly with norovirus would likely be dehydrated. He could draw bloods, give anti-emetics, put up IV lines and keep them comfortable. Cardiac patients were his speciality, but Avery was always prepared to help out when things were busy. And apparently so was Robyn.

He was a little intrigued. The fleeing surgeon was not unique. Once most doctors moved to their specialist areas, they didn't like to cross into any other territory.

He moved over to cubicle seven. He could hear Robyn's Scottish accent immediately. He moved his head to see through the gap in the curtains. She'd obviously changed out of her running clothes from earlier and was wearing a knee-length shirt-style red dress, belted at the waist, and flat black shoes. The colour surprised him, but looked good on her. His brain instantly told him that it was ridiculous to think people with red hair wouldn't wear red clothes. Her hair was pulled back from her face with a black headband. Her traditional white coat was nowhere in sight.

She was pointing to the screen of the ultrasound machine. 'This shows the flow of blood through your heart.' He could see exactly what she was focusing on—one of the heart valves.

'Tell me exactly when you've felt short of breath,' she asked the young man.

He squirmed a little. 'I've put on some weight. I'm not sure why. I'm still playing basketball. But I just don't have the same energy. I feel short of breath after ten minutes of play.'

Robyn spoke. 'You can come in,' she said in a low voice without turning her head from her patient.

Avery gave a small start—embarrassed that she'd realised he was there. He stepped in through the curtains and gave a nod to the young man. 'Hi there, I'm Avery Smith, one of the nurses from the cardiac unit.' He turned to Robyn. 'I came down from the unit to see if you needed any help.'

She gave him a slightly nervous smile. 'I paged Dr Anker. Can you check if he's answered and he's on his way?'

Avery nodded and headed back out to the nurses' station, in time to see Dr Anker—in his golf clothes—walking from the opposite direction. He'd seen this irritated face on a few occasions. Dr Anker was a good cardiologist, but was an older man, and there was no getting away from the fact he could be chauvinistic at times.

He nodded at Avery. 'Good, finally someone with sense. Did you tell her she shouldn't page me?'

Avery straightened up. 'Actually, I think you'll be interested in the patient. He looks as if he has valve disease. It's a good catch by our new doctor.'

Dr Anker gave Avery a hard stare for a few moments. Avery could swear he could almost hear the man's brain ticking.

Avery was sure about what he'd seen on the screen in the cubicle—just as he was sure Robyn had been. She'd been right to argue with Paediatrics about not discharging this young man.

Dr Anker drew in a deep breath and gave a nod. 'In that case, let me see.'

Avery led him down the corridor. As they approached they could hear Robyn talking to someone else. 'Was Simon ever sick as a child?' she was asking.

Dr Anker drew back the curtain and frowned. Robyn was video-calling an adult on a phone. Avery guessed it was Simon's mom.

She waited until she got an affirmative reply, then turned at the noise. Her cheeks flushed, and Avery could see her starting to get nervous. She handed over an electronic chart to Dr Anker.

'Simon, this is Dr Anker, the specialist doctor I told you I'd called. He'll check you over and will likely want to talk to your mom too.'

Dr Anker was already flicking through the electronic report. 'Chest X-ray, blood work, ECG.' He looked up sharply. 'Where's his echocardiogram?'

'I've just completed it,' Robyn said quickly. 'I've not reported it yet, but the recording is here for you to view.'

Dr Anker pulled his stethoscope from his neck. 'In a second.' His slightly gruff manner disappeared and he turned to his patient, an old-time charm appearing. Within a few minutes he'd listened to Simon's heart, lungs and reviewed his echocardiogram, before going on to ask Robyn to call Simon's mother back.

Avery gave Robyn a reassuring smile. Was that a slight tremor in her hand?

She'd done everything right. She shouldn't be worried at all.

Dr Anker turned to her, as if he'd read Avery's mind. 'Good catch, Dr Callaghan. I can see that the other doctor was prepared to send Simon home without carrying out so many investigations. Cardiac conditions can easily be missed in teenagers.'

He turned on a dazzling smile to Simon's mother. 'You're on your way in? Good. I'm going to arrange for Simon to come upstairs to our specialist unit. I have some staff who specialise in teenagers and I'll assign one of them to Simon's care.'

He made a few scrawls with an electronic pen on Simon's chart, then gave a few other brief instructions.

Robyn stepped outside after Dr Anker to get some final details and scribble some quick notes. Dr Anker disappeared fairly quickly and Avery looked at Robyn. 'Paeds really wanted to discharge him?'

She nodded. 'They said the shortness of breath was due to his weight.'

Avery tried not to look surprised. 'Wow. They didn't look past that? They didn't consider anything else?'

She shook her head. 'I came down for something else and just heard them chatting about Simon. His report of his sudden weight gain seemed odd to me. As was his sudden shortness of breath.' She lowered her voice. 'I didn't get as much time as I'd have liked on his echocardiogram, but his heart valve is diseased. I'm guessing undiagnosed rheumatic fever.'

Avery nodded. 'I think you're right. We've

had a few adults in their mid-twenties with rheumatic fever in the unit.'

Robyn seemed to be calming down. 'Okay,' she said, as if she was reassuring herself. She closed her eyes for a second. 'Everyone told me not to page Dr Anker. But it was the only way I could persuade the ER doc that Simon should stay. As for the paediatrician, I don't think he'll talk to me again.'

'Don't worry about that,' said Avery. 'You did a good job.'

She nodded her head then looked at Avery for a moment and finally smiled. 'Thank you,' she said. 'I'll call up to the unit to arrange to transfer Simon up. Unless you can take him?'

He went to answer but she jumped back in. 'Sorry, I didn't mean it like that. I'd take him up myself, but I said I'd stay and give them a hand down here.'

He gave her a smile. 'Me too.'

'Oh.' She looked surprised, and then almost laughed and shook her head. 'I'll make that call, then.'

Avery was painfully aware of where Robyn was for the next few hours. Every flash of red hair or red dress seemed to imprint on his brain. She was like the ultimate distraction and he couldn't entirely work out why. One hour inevitably turned into two, then almost three.

He looked after seven elderly patients from the care home, all dehydrated, some confused, but he took bloods, a history where he could, put up IV lines, and rolled endless commodes in and out of the cubicle curtains. Norovirus was never pleasant, and was highly infectious. Avery was careful to ensure he wore protective clothing and equipment that he changed between every patient. It was hot and uncomfortable down in the ER, and the protective equipment made that even worse. He found water jugs and glasses for all seven of the older patients and took the time to make sure they were all sipping water on a regular basis.

As he was finishing all his notes one of the elderly women started to cry out. She reached towards Avery. 'Paul,' she murmured. 'Paul, where have you been?' Her voice was weak and crackly. Avery knew she was confused by the dehydration, and by the urinary tract infection she also had. He sat down next to her, lifting a glass with water, and putting in a straw and holding it up to her mouth.

'I'm here now,' he said quietly. 'Take a sip of water.'

She obeyed and settled down, holding one of his hands and stroking it. Avery knew it would only cause her more distress if he told her he wasn't the Paul she thought he was. So, he sat with her and talked softly. Listening to her stories and nodding in agreement. After a while she laid her head back on the pillow and went to sleep.

At one point, he thought he saw a flash of a red dress again and wondered if Robyn had finished with her patient. But he didn't want to move from his position until he was sure that his elderly lady was completely asleep. Avery took another few moments, going back around checking all the other patients he'd looked after, making sure they were comfortable. By the time he'd finished all the charting, Michael appeared behind him.

'You've been an angel today,' he said quickly. 'I can't tell you how much I appreciate it. A lot of people would have been reluctant to help— particularly with anything that can be infectious.'

Avery held up his hands. 'All of them are really quite sick. I was happy to help. Is there anything else you want me to do?'

Michael shook his head. 'We've taken enough of your time. Your doctor too—she's been amazing. She can certainly fly through the patients, can't she?'

Avery's skin prickled a little. Some people would see that as a compliment. But others?

They might see it as a sign of shoddy or care-less work.

'I'll just go and check on her,' he said dis-tractedly, his eyes going to the whiteboard to see which patient she was examining.

As he walked along the corridor towards her, things immediately got more complicated. She was talking to a disdainful-looking young man, a notebook in hand, a stethoscope around his neck, and a pristine white coat. A clear sign of a medical student. There was something about him that Avery couldn't quite put his finger on. He gave the student a nod as he approached. 'Avery Smith,' he said as introduction.

The student gave him a half-hearted glance but didn't reply.

Robyn continued. 'Let's go over the details again.'

The medical student appeared confident. 'The ER manager told us that around thirty per cent of people who attend shouldn't be at an ER. It costs millions of dollars every year. We need to filter them out.'

Avery saw Robyn's eyes light up with inter-est. 'Go on,' she said. There was something in her voice, in the tone, that the medical student didn't catch. But Avery did. He wanted to warn the young man to tread very carefully. But it was already too late.

'I checked over Mr Runo's symptoms. They were vague. He just said he didn't feel right. His right eyelid was a little droopy. But it wasn't pronounced. He had full movement in his right hand, arm and leg. Nothing to indicate he'd had a stroke, or even a trans ischaemic attack. His blood pressure and heart rate were both slightly raised, but not clinically worrying. He said something about his face not sweating—but how could he even know that? There's air conditioning in the ER. There was no confusion. He's orientated to time and place. No headache, no nausea. No signs of anything else. It all just seemed—' he threw up his hands '—a whole lot of nothing.'

Avery was already reaching into his pocket for his pen torch as Robyn spoke the very telling words. 'Were his pupils equal and reactive?' She made the question sound normal.

The student looked momentarily surprised. He patted his pockets, clearly realising he didn't have a pen torch. Avery handed over his own. 'I didn't check,' said the student.

'Could you check now?' asked Robyn. The edge to her voice was becoming very distinct.

The student disappeared behind the set of curtains. Avery gave Robyn a careful glance. 'We were all students once,' he said quietly.

'Were we all complete tools too?' she replied.

Avery frowned, trying to make sense of the words. 'So, in Scotland, if someone is a "tool"—that means?'

'Insert the word of your choice,' she said briskly. 'Fool. Prat. Imbecile.'

Avery held up his hand. 'Tough crowd.'

Robyn stared impatiently at the curtains, waiting for the student to emerge again. 'What are you doing here anyway?'

'I came to see if you needed a hand with anything,' he said, giving her a bright smile. 'You know, after you told me I abandoned you here the last time.' He looked at the curtains too. 'But it seems as if I should stay as a protective shield for the medical student whose name I don't even know yet.'

Robyn gave him a dirty look. 'I've waited long enough.' She swept the curtains aside and stepped inside the cubicle.

'How are Mr Runo's eyes?' she asked.

The student turned round. His earlier cocky demeanour had vanished. He wasn't looking quite so confident now. It was clear he was feeling defensive.

'Well, it's hard to tell. But one of his pupils might be slightly constricted.'

'I see. Can you think of any conditions that you can link the symptoms to that you've found today?'

He blinked. His opened then closed his mouth as if trying to find an answer, but he shook his head. 'Nothing seems clear enough to make a definitive diagnosis.'

Avery saw something flash across her eyes. She took a deep breath and pulled her own pen torch out of her pocket. 'Watch, and learn,' she said as she walked through the curtains.

Avery followed after the student. He couldn't fault Robyn's handling of Mr Runo. She was pleasant and professional. She asked questions without causing alarm, specifying symptoms and their length, and gathering as much history as she could. Once she'd examined Mr Runo herself, she sat in a chair at the edge of the bed.

'Mr Runo, you've got a fairly unusual condition. It has a couple of names. One is Horner's Syndrome, the other is oculo-sympathetic paresis.' She gave him a smile. 'Yes, I know, it's a confusing name. What it really means is that one of the nerves that feeds into your face is being affected somehow. That's why your eyelid is drooping, your pupil is constricted, and you're not sweating on one side of your face.' She took out a mirror and gave him a few moments to look at his own pupil. 'I'm glad you came in today,' she said reassuringly. 'My job, as your doctor, is to carry out some tests to find out why your nerve is affected. Once we know, we can look at getting some treatment for you.'

She gave him a gentle pat on the hand. 'You'll need to stay a few days. Can we contact someone for you?'

Avery whipped out a pen and took a note of the name and number Mr Runo said while Robyn kept talking.

They left the cubicle a few minutes later and Robyn walked the student into one of the nearby treatment rooms. 'Tell me what you know about Horner's Syndrome.'

'Never heard of it,' said the student bluntly. 'Just know what you said to the patient.'

Robyn nodded her head slowly. 'What do you think could cause an issue with a facial nerve, then?'

'A disc problem. Swelling. An injury.' It was clear he was grasping at straws. 'It seems minor. The symptoms were difficult to spot.'

Avery felt his stomach clench. Paz Memorial was a renowned teaching hospital. They were used to students here—from all disciplines. Most were keen, pleasant and anxious to learn. Only occasionally did they get a few that were on the arrogant side who secretly thought they knew best. And weren't particularly prepared to learn. Avery could also sense an element of chauvinism from this student. His body language towards Robyn was causing small alarm bells to ring for Avery. He clearly didn't like being taught by a woman.

Avery might only have been around Robyn a few days, but he knew this was unlikely to end well—not with this straight-talking doctor.

'Let's be really clear,' she said, her accent strong. 'You potentially could have sent Mr Runo home. If you had, you should know that his Horner's Syndrome could be caused by a variety of tumours, a carotid artery dissection, or encephalitis—to name just a few.' She held up the electronic chart. 'If you had, the physical findings that you recorded, but missed the importance of, could have caused you to spend a long time in court, and risk the medical licence you are hoping to gain.'

Silence. Avery was thankful.

'Who is your supervisor?'

'You're only covering down here. I shouldn't even be working alongside you.' The words were spat out with unhidden indignance. Avery winced.

Robyn held up her hand. 'Stop. Now.' Her voice was very firm, very clear.

'I was going to suggest to your supervisor that you use Mr Runo as one of your patient cases and follow through on his investigations and treatment. Horner's Syndrome is rare.

There is much to learn here. Most of your student colleagues would have been jealous that you've seen a case and, potentially, got to write it up as one of your learning achievements.' She put one hand on her hip. 'But it seems I'll be having an alternative conversation with your supervisor about your attitude.'

The medical student seemed to realise his mistake. But instead of immediately apologising, he maintained his superior demeanour and shook his head. 'Robyn,' he said condescendingly, as if he actually knew her, 'I think you've misunderstood.'

Avery stepped between the two. 'I don't think there has been any misunderstanding. In order to do well at Paz Memorial, you have to want to learn—and you have to show respect to your patients, and your colleagues. It's time for you to stop talking. Go to the library. You have some reading to do. I'll speak to the ER manager and let him know where you are.'

The disdain on the student's face was clear. 'You can't tell me what to do. You're just a *nurse*.' He spat the word out as if it were unpleasant.

Avery kept calm. He'd dealt with angry patients and relatives in the past—they didn't faze him. He'd also dealt with similar students. Sometimes arrogance was a front. Sometimes people who seemed disdainful were anxious, or worried. Avery was always painfully aware he didn't know what lives people lived away from the hospital. And yet he couldn't shake the feeling of just…something familiar about this student.

The student was clutching his ID badge in his hand but Avery couldn't make out the name. 'You need to leave,' Avery said firmly. He was at least four inches taller than the student, and while he'd never use his size to intimidate someone, it also didn't hurt that he went to the gym a few times a week.

The student turned abruptly and strode down the corridor. There was purpose to his steps. 'He's going to complain about us,' said Avery matter-of-factly.

'He'll have to be fast to beat me,' said Robyn. She turned on her heel, striding down the corridor to the ER manager's office.

She knocked once and entered. The timing could be better. Last thing a manager wanted to hear when a place was extremely busy was that they had a student who could be trouble.

Avery waited outside. He wasn't the type to get involved in any kind of pile-on, but he would support a colleague if asked to give his version of events.

He could hear low voices inside. Two minutes later Jon stuck his head out of the door, starting when he saw Avery waiting. 'Perfect, you're still here, Avery—did the student miss the diagnosis?'

Avery nodded.

'Was he rude?'

'Definitely.'

Jon sighed and ran his hand through his hair. 'Do I need to take him off the floor?'

Avery shook his head. 'If he has the capacity, he should learn from his counterparts. But he needs proper supervision. I know you're busy, and I know he would have run his findings past another doctor before discharging the patient, but...' Avery stopped. 'No. Actually, I'm not sure he would have done that. He was over-confident. He also has a lack of respect for nursing and female medical staff.' He put a hand on Jon's shoulder. 'Good luck with that one.'

'So, Dr Callaghan isn't overreacting?'

Avery shook his head. 'No. She's definitely not.'

Jon lowered his head and put his hand on his hips. 'And it would have to be him, wouldn't it?'

Robyn walked out of the door beside them both. 'Who?' she asked.

Jon lifted his hand. 'Nothing. It doesn't matter.' He gave them both a resigned look. 'Thanks for letting me know. I'll deal with him.'

As they walked back down the corridor, Robyn looked at Avery. 'Do you get the feeling Jon didn't tell us everything?'

Avery sighed. 'I'm not sure. Maybe he's just tired or overwhelmed by the rush today.' He looked sideways at Robyn. 'Let's grab some food before we go back upstairs. We'll have missed the roster for breaks and I don't want to go all day without eating.'

'Me either,' she agreed.

As they walked through the corridors to the cafeteria he could see the serious expression on her face. Robyn was pretty, but her face was often marred by a frown. He knew better than to tell a woman to smile—not if he wanted to see another day—so he took the conversation another way.

'It was nice that you offered to help out in the ER today. Not many would have done that. You had two really good catches today. The teenager, and the Horner's Syndrome. Not everyone would have picked up on those—particularly when it's not your speciality.'

Now she did smile as they pushed open the cafeteria doors. 'I told you. I'm smart. Didn't you believe me?'

He thought back to her story about how many

applicants there had been to her programme. He had actually believed her, because Robyn Callaghan gave him the distinct impression that she was an entirely truthful human being—she wouldn't waste time with lies.

'I did believe you,' he admitted, 'but sometimes believing something and witnessing it with your own eyes are two entirely different things.'

She was still smiling as they approached the counter and grabbed a tray. She selected a diet drink, a tuna-fish salad and, after much deliberation, a chocolate bar. She sighed. 'I miss my UK chocolate. Things just don't taste the same over here.'

Avery kept pace with her, picking up a bottle of water, then letting out a groan and grabbing a grilled-cheese sandwich from a fresh tray one of the staff had just put on the serving plates. Robyn gave him a smile. 'It's the one food you can eat the whole world over.'

He nodded, looking at her salad. 'I should get the same as you, but one whiff of the grilled cheese and I knew I was gone.'

They paid for their food and sat down at a table facing out onto the courtyard.

A small gust of air breezed by them and he got a hint of something spicy with hints of orange. It must have been her perfume—and he didn't recognise it.

'Did you get to finish all your notes on the Horner's case?'

Robyn nodded. 'I was recording as I went along and I'd already sent a handover note to both physicians who'll be taking over his care.' She took a forkful of her salad. 'But I'll go back and chase both. Our boy Simon will be easy to follow up, because he'll be in our unit.' She paused for a moment. 'Think I've made an enemy of Dr Anker?'

Avery pulled a face. 'Honestly? It's hard to say. He's a bit of a Jekyll and Hyde character, and you never know which one you're going to get. Most of the nurses in the unit try and go on a break when it's time for him to do his rounds.' He gave her a broad smile. 'But the most important rule is never to page him when he's playing golf—even if he is the senior doctor on call.'

Robyn groaned. 'Well, that's strike one against me already, then.'

Avery held up a hand. 'It could go two ways. He might be impressed you stood your ground with the paediatrician, and picked up a condition in a teenage boy that means he can be treated. There is a chance he could like that about you.'

'Or…?' She said the word because there were clearly unanswered elements hanging in the air.

Avery finished chewing part of his grilled cheese sandwich. 'Or he'll just remember you as the pesky doc who ruined his best game of golf ever. You'll get all the grunt work to do for the rest of your time here.'

Robyn leaned her head on one hand. She tapped her fingers on the table. 'I can live with grunt work. That's not so bad.'

Avery laughed. 'Oh, no. Dr Anker's grunt work is legendary. He once made a doctor who'd annoyed him pull five hundred random case notes of past patients to audit the medicines used.'

'Was it for a study?'

Avery shook his head.

'Because, if it was for a study, about finding best outcomes after procedures, that would be good. It could be written up as a research paper.'

'Stop trying to make things seem better. There was no research paper. You'll just need to wait to see what personality he's wearing later today or tomorrow.'

She gave a sad kind of smile. 'Medicine would be great, if it wasn't for people.'

'You sound like my old charge nurse.'

Robyn looked up. Her blue eyes meeting his.

It was the first time he'd got a real look at her. Her dark red hair was smooth and shiny, her pale skin, with a few fine freckles on her nose, and dark blue eyes complemented her tones. There were no lines on her skin yet. She wore a little make-up, including striking red lipstick that matched her dress.

If he'd seen her someplace else, he'd have thought she was some kind of actress or model. But no, she was here, in Paz Memorial, in his home town.

Her accent was lilting to listen to. He still had to concentrate on occasion to understand every word, but he loved that everyone knew exactly where she came from, as soon as she opened her mouth.

'What did your old charge nurse say?' she asked.

'Oh, Marie said that work was great—apart from managing staff. She said there was always drama, always in-fighting, and holiday squabbles. Marie hated that it got in the way of patient care. She ended up retiring early.'

Robyn looked thoughtful. 'Was that good, or bad?'

It was an interesting question. Had Marie been too jaded to do her job well?

'Both,' he admitted. 'Bad, in that Marie was a wonderful nurse, great with relatives and patients, and I learned a lot from her. Her teaching skills were impeccable. But good in that a disgruntled staff member complained about her. Went to HR because Marie wasn't sympathetic to her apparent health issues.'

'Did she have health issues?'

'Not that anyone knew of. Plus, this woman had a history of moving from place to place and causing trouble. But for Marie, it was the last straw.'

'And how is she?'

Avery sat back. 'What makes you think I know?'

Robyn shook her head, pushing her salad away and unwrapping her chocolate bar. 'Because you do, don't you? You just spoke about a colleague you like and admired. It's clear you think she was shafted in some way. So, now she's retired, how is she?'

Avery nodded. 'She makes a great Sunday dinner. She helps out at a soup kitchen with me a couple of times a month, and at the free clinic. And she looks ten years younger.'

'I knew it.' Robyn looked triumphant. Avery leaned over and snapped off a square of her chocolate. 'Hey!' She wrinkled her nose. 'Why do I think you make a habit of this?'

Avery shrugged. 'I have no idea.'

Robyn looked at him curiously. 'You mentioned me helping out in the ER today. But you came down and helped out too. I saw you with some of those elderly patients.'

He wondered what else she was going to say. He gave a shake of his head. 'Of course, I helped out. The place was going crazy.' He decided to be truthful. 'I have some experience with surgical patients, and I did spend some time in the ER, theatres, general medical unit and care of elderly when I was doing my nurse training. But I'm no expert. When I offer to help I'm always careful not to step outside of what I know. Today, I knew I could take care of the elderly patients, do bloods, put up IVs, run tests, and make sure they were comfortable.'

'I saw you sitting with one of them for a while. Talking to her, telling her a story, and holding her hand.'

Avery nodded in acknowledgement. It *had* been Robyn that had walked past when he'd been looking after the elderly patient. 'She was upset. She has dementia. She thought I was her husband.' He drew in a long breath. 'Of course, I was going to spend time with her. The ER is overwhelming. Her confusion was heightened with the dehydration and infection she was suffering from. It was nice to take a bit of time with her. You don't always get that opportunity when places are so busy.'

Robyn gave him a contemplative look. 'Maybe you shouldn't have specialised in cardiac, maybe you should have considered care of the elderly.'

Something flashed through his brain. 'I'm not built for it. I find it difficult enough helping at the free clinic, and at the soup kitchen. With the older folk? I get too attached, and too frustrated with the lack of investment in services for our older patients, aids to keep them safely at home, in an environment they are familiar with, and even more exasperated by the "granny dumping".'

Robyn gave a shudder, clearly in sympathy. The act of an older relative being left at an ER by other members of the family, who didn't stay, was not entirely unusual to either of them. 'It's not so bad back in the UK, but it does still happen. Although healthcare is free, social care carries a cost. Some local authorities struggle to provide packages of care to keep people at home, usually due to a high turnover of staff, so, on occasion, it happens there too.'

He shook his head. 'And that's why I couldn't consider elderly care. I'd get too angry. Plus, the cardiac stuff always fascinated me. There's so much to learn, so many developments, and new techniques and drugs all the time. It's definitely the right place to be. And Paz Memorial is world-renowned as a centre of excellence. Why would I want to be anywhere else?'

Robyn leaned back and stifled a yawn. 'Sorry,' she said quickly. 'I haven't had a proper night's sleep since I got here.'

He was curious. 'Is something wrong with your accommodation?'

Robyn held up her hands. 'I started a little later than everyone else. There was a mix-up with my working visa, and by the time I got here all the rooms had been assigned except the one I got. It's right above the back entrance to the kitchen. I can tell you that the milk gets delivered at three a.m., the farm supplies get delivered around four a.m., and the baked goods around five a.m. If I'm hot and open my window it just amplifies the noise of all the delivery trucks. If I don't get some sleep soon, I'm likely to kill someone.' She must have caught his expression because she quickly added, 'Not because of bad medical practice. Just because sleep deprivation makes me decidedly cranky. I'll probably fight someone to the death over the last bar of chocolate.'

He tried not to smile too widely. 'Heaven help the person that gets between you and your chocolate.'

Robyn picked up the bar and held it to her chest. 'Don't you know it?' She glanced at the clock. 'We'd better get back to work.' She shot him a sideways glance as they headed to the exit. 'Don't want to get labelled a slacker as well as grumpy.' There was a twinkle in her eye.

She headed up the stairs before him and he made sure to fix his gaze on her shoes rather than anywhere far more distracting. Robyn Callaghan was proving more than a little interesting and he had a horrible feeling that his friend Serena knew him better than he knew himself.

CHAPTER THREE

'HOW ON EARTH can a medical student get away
with that?'

It was a few days later and Robyn was finally getting the hang of all the processes in the
cardiac department. While she was always confident in her medical skills, learning the processes somewhere new always took time. She
often found herself lying in bed at night wondering if she'd ticked all the boxes on a hand-
written bloodwork form, or if she'd pressed
the final electronic button on an order for a
test. Last thing she wanted was for a patient's
care to be delayed or compromised because
she hadn't managed to find her way around
all the systems.

She hated to admit it, but Avery had been
more than helpful. He'd gone through all the
electronic processes with her and even given
her a checklist for her pocket. She was quite
sure the folks around here were still calling her

Dr Grumpy, but Robyn was concentrating on the medicine, not the people skills.

She walked over to join the staff gossiping. Lia, one of the nurses, was rolling her eyes. 'No one's said anything, but I guess it's got something to do with who he actually is.'

'You mean how much money his family's got and who he knows on the board,' another nurse wisecracked as she walked by.

Robyn couldn't help but be intrigued, clearly a mistake as Lia turned to her. 'You know all about it, Robyn. Tell us more.'

'More about what?'

'The medical student who messed up in the ER, but is still walking around telling everyone that he requires minimal supervision and that no one will stifle his learning.'

Robyn waited a few seconds for the rage to rise, then fall again. 'I imagine he can say whatever he wants. All medical students will mess up at some point. It's normal.' She licked her lips and connected with Lia's inquisitive gaze. 'It's what they learn from their mistakes that makes or breaks them as a doctor.'

Lia nodded. 'But your guy is telling all the other students that he was initially told he required supervision but his uncle has intervened.'

'Who's his uncle?'

Everyone stared at her. 'What?' she said. 'What have I missed?'

Lia patted her arm gently. 'His uncle is our chief executive, Mr Paz.'

Her stomach did a skydive, then a somersault, then a backflip, but she refused to let anyone know. Robyn was an expert at the deadpan face.

'It doesn't matter who his uncle is. He's a medical student and they all need supervision—whether he likes it or not. I've never met a programme director who would let the overall basis of their programme be compromised by any kind of influence like nepotism—' she glanced at the other wisecracking nurse who'd stopped walking '—or money.'

Robyn gave a shrug. 'Paz Memorial has a great reputation as a teaching hospital. That won't be risked.' She shook her head. 'He'll just be shooting his mouth off because someone found out what happened down there.' She raised her eyebrows. 'I haven't discussed it with anyone. I'd never do that. I'd never gossip about a student when I know they are working in our hospital.'

She witnessed a few embarrassed exchanges of glances, along with some hostile glares. 'I'm going to get a coffee. Anyone want one?'

She wasn't normally so hospitable, but she

was trying to make a point. There was a general shake of heads and Robyn started to walk back to the staffroom, but changed her mind and descended the stairs to the machine in the cafeteria. They had a coffee bar and she ordered a skimmed extra-shot latte. Her heart was already racing, so an extra shot of coffee wouldn't make much difference.

Robyn climbed the stairs again and nestled herself in one of the offices, reviewing some patient notes and ordering some extra tests. Once she had finished, she exited the hospital programme, and surfed the Internet looking for a little more about the Paz family.

It was a large family, with lots of branches, and she couldn't quite work out where the medical student potentially could fit. Maybe it was just hospital gossip.

Her heart had finally stilled to a dull roar. She'd already caught the attention of Mr Paz by throwing him out of a cubicle in the ER. Now, if his relative complained that she'd highlighted him to his programme supervisor, she could find herself on a shaky peg.

The anger that she'd found so easy to quell earlier started to bubble again. Robyn had always been quick to flare with temper, but that was rarely visible to anyone else. She usually controlled it well. The only time it threatened to bubble over was when money and privilege were involved. Living on the wrong side of financial privilege for most of her life had given her what some might consider a skewed view on the unfairness of it all—one that she'd never been shy about vocalising.

Too many students from private schools were regularly reported as getting into medical schools—even when students from public schools had scored the same results in their exams. They had lower acceptance rates that a variety of excuses were made around.

Robyn had worked exceptionally hard to get where she was—despite her address in one of the most deprived areas of Scotland. She'd tried hard not to be envious of her fellow students who'd attended university with huge trust funds that had meant they had the best accommodation and didn't have to worry about eating or paying any bills.

Robyn had spent most of her life going without, so it had been nothing new to her. It was her normal. When she'd got a job doing late nights at a pub a few miles away from the university, she'd lived in constant fear of someone recognising her, and reporting her. The university had a rule that none of their students could take part-time jobs while studying. And while it was a nice idea that students could spend all their time and effort studying, the sad fact of life was that not everyone could afford to live that lifestyle.

'Hey,' a voice came from the door. 'Could you have a look at Mr Burns for me? He's getting tachycardic and his oxygen sats have gone down.'

Robyn was on her feet in an instant, already unwinding her stethoscope from her neck. She followed the worried nurse through to the cardiac unit where Mr Burns was situated. She'd read his notes. He'd had a whole host of cardiac issues for the last few years and had been admitted to the unit on multiple occasions.

The nurse was right. His colour was slightly off. Not blue. Not deathly pale. But definitely the start of something.

She glanced at the monitor. Heart rate one hundred and ten. Oxygen level ninety-one.

Avery appeared at her side. 'What's happening?'

She knew that he was familiar with Mr Burns and had looked after him on many occasions. He stepped around to the other side of the bed, and automatically helped Mr Burns to sit up, allowing Robyn to sound his chest and back.

She gave a slight nod when she was finished,

and adjusted the pillows to let Mr Burns settle in a more upright position.

'Let's order a chest X-ray and get some bloods,' she said with a nod to the other nurse.

'Don't worry, Mr Burns, we'll look after you.'

She scribbled some notes and moved over to the nurses' station, asking for the phone. Avery appeared beside her as she paged Mr Burns' regular cardiologist.

He raised his eyebrows at her and she pulled a pad from her pocket, writing him a cryptic note: PE? He groaned and nodded. It wasn't uncommon for people with cardiac conditions to throw off a clot due to the fact their heart wasn't pumping blood around the body quite the way it should. Clots could form anywhere, but in this case Robyn suspected it was in the branch of one of his lungs, meaning that now they were compromised, and couldn't absorb oxygen properly.

She spoke in a low voice to Mr Burns' regular doctor, telling him her findings, the tests she'd already ordered and asking whether he would prefer a pulmonary angiogram, a CT or VQ scan. All could play a role in diagnosing a pulmonary embolism, and Robyn didn't know these doctors well enough to know what their preferences would be.

He surprised her, telling her he would attend himself and decide at that point. Some of the specialists rarely attended in an emergency, but it appeared that Dr Shad was different.

'Have you met him yet?' asked Avery as she replaced the receiver.

She shook her head, wondering if she should even ask the question of what he was like.

But it was as if someone read her mind. 'The man's a dream,' came a voice at the other side of her. Rue, one of the physios, was smiling. 'Always pleasant, always put his patients first.' She put her hand on her chest. 'If I ever end up in here, that man *better* be my doctor.'

'Can't get a better recommendation than that,' Robyn said, smiling. And it was true. Doctors and nurses were the same the world over. They could list who they did and they *didn't* want to take care of them, in any place they'd worked.

Robyn looked around, suddenly self-conscious. Once they got to know her, would any of the staff here want her to be their doctor in case of emergency? She swallowed, her throat dry. She'd like to think so, but she honestly wasn't sure. Avery, meantime, was already talking to a patient who'd just pushed their buzzer. He had his trademark wide smile on his face. Mr Sunshine. It seemed to be his natural instinct.

Robyn had been told before that she had a resting bitch face. Charming. It was the same person who'd first tried to charm her by telling her she looked like a famous cartoon princess, and then tried to come on to her. When she'd been unimpressed, she'd then received the ultimate compliment regarding her normal expression. She'd been self-conscious about it ever since. And that was so not like her.

She watched Avery for a few minutes because she just couldn't help it. He was so comfortable in his own skin. If he knew how handsome he was, he certainly didn't play on it. Avery was very down-to-earth and went out of his way to take the time to talk to people. She hadn't heard another member of staff say a bad word about him.

In a way he kind of unnerved her. Too good-looking. Too friendly. Too sexy. Too easy to chat to. Too nice. Too much fun. She really needed to get a life.

Robyn sighed. She glanced at the clock. She was due to be off duty, and she really, really wanted to get to sleep. But there was no way she was leaving now she knew one of the senior doctors was coming.

'I'm going to do some checks on other patients,' she told the charge nurse, 'Can you give me a shout when Dr Shad appears?'

The nurse nodded and Robyn went to follow up on some other test results, and to check in on Hal Delaney, the man who'd had a cardiac arrest at the front door.

He was in a luxury private room in a special part of the unit, with his own private nurses and his own chef. It was likely that he only wanted his specialist doctor to see him, but Robyn always liked to check up on any patient she'd been involved with.

She knocked on the door and went in. 'Hi, Mr Delaney. I'm Robyn Callaghan, one of the doctors who looked after you downstairs. I came in to see how you were doing.'

The man was reading an old-fashioned newspaper. They were nowhere near as popular as they used to be, with most people reading their news online now.

He looked up and put his paper down on his bed sheets. His head tilted slightly to the side, then she could see the recognition in his face. He let out a hearty laugh. 'The red-haired fire demon. I wondered if I'd actually imagined you.'

Robyn blinked. She'd been called an angel before, but demon was a first.

But now Hal Delaney was wagging his finger. 'It's the accent. It imprinted in my brain.' He held out his hand towards her. 'Whereabouts in Scotland are you from?'

'Near Glasgow,' she said, shaking his hand gently.

'Scotland.' He sighed, putting his hands up in the air. 'I think someone bought me a peerage there as a birthday gift. Beautiful country.'

All the hairs on her neck stood on end. She'd known Mr Delaney was likely to be rich from his private room and service. But now she knew for sure. Maybe she was supposed to be amused by that anecdote, but, funnily enough, some rich man buying a peerage in her country as a kind of joke did nothing for her.

'I'm glad to hear that you're doing well, Mr Delaney. How much longer do you expect to be in?'

She hadn't looked at his notes—not quite sure what the etiquette was in the hospital for patients who were being cared for in a different way.

He didn't answer, just rested back against his pillows, and kept smiling at her, shaking his head. His monitor was to his side and she could see his heart rate and last blood-pressure recording. If she was asked to place a bet, she'd say that Mr Delaney would be getting a pacemaker sometime soon.

'I'm just excited to meet someone who had the nerve to tell Leo Paz to get out the room. Most people are terrified of him.'

'They are?' Robyn tried to hide the most enormous gulp.

'Oh, yes, even though I was sick, I was delighted you had the balls to tell him off.'

The door opened and a support worker came in with a large carafe of coffee. 'Is that decaf?' Robyn couldn't help but ask the question.

The support worker shook their head. So, Robyn shook hers. 'Bring back some decaf, please.'

Mr Delaney started to object but Robyn moved closer to his bed and pointed to his monitor. 'Your heart rate is tachycardic but irregular. You must feel the palpitations?'

He frowned, but nodded.

'Did your doctor suggest modifications to your diet until he has things stable?'

Mr Delaney's frown deepened but he nodded again. 'But I pay my own chef.'

She bristled at the entitlement and the fact he'd ignored the instructions given by his doctor. But decided to tackle this a different way.

Robyn gave him a smile. 'So, just like I had the balls to tell Mr Paz to leave while I treated you, I have the balls to tell you to spend the next few days following the instructions of your doctor.' She tapped the monitor. 'Your heart rate is very irregular. You're going to need this treated. I really don't want to have to answer an arrest page for you again.'

She paused, looking at him to let the words sink in, then taking another breath. She could frame this as a challenge. 'There's lots of great decaf versions out there—and I'm sure you're happy to pay for the best. Why don't you sample a few versions to see if you can find one that tastes just as good as the brand you normally drink?'

He mumbled under his breath, clearly used to getting his own way unchallenged.

The support worker came back in with another large pot of coffee. It smelled just as good as the last.

'Thank you,' said Robyn as they set it down then left again.

Mr Delaney was giving her a hard stare through heavy lids. She folded her arms across her chest. 'I want you to know that as a child I was unmatched in stare-out duels.'

He blinked and let out a snort. 'Are all Scots women like you?'

'You should know. Don't you own a peerage?' she shot back without hesitation.

He poured his coffee into what she assumed

was a fine bone-china teacup and plate. 'I like you,' he said.

'You should. I helped save your life. Take care of it, Mr Delaney. I want to hear that you've lived a long, happy and healthy life.'

She gave him a wave and exited the room, just as the support worker appeared with a plate full of delicious, clearly freshly baked cakes. Robyn sighed and plucked the top one from the plate with a wink, and the startled support worker stared at her. 'I'm helping with his diet,' Robyn explained as she walked back down the corridor nibbling the delicious raspberry and coconut sponge.

It seemed that the rumours were true. Dr Shad was a delight and gave Robyn faith that not all senior doctors were fierce and a bit conceited. By the time she was finished on the unit, all she really wanted to do was lie down in her bed.

But the muggy evening air was too warm, so she changed into shorts and flowery top and took a walk down along the front, staring at the giant naval vessels, then working her way across and into the Gaslamp district. It really was one of her favourite parts of San Diego. The atmosphere was always friendly. People seemed relaxed. Music drifted out from a few of the bars. Several of the restaurants had tables outside and the smells were nothing short of tantalising.

Robyn considered her bank balance. While she was surviving, she would never describe her bank balance as healthy. She lived pay cheque to pay cheque. She constantly had to help out her parents back at home—neither of them had ever held down regular jobs. Both just seemed to drift from one low-paying job to another, with no built-in benefits and frequently being laid off at short notice.

She glanced at a few menus on the restaurant windows. She had no qualms about going in and eating on her own—she was quite comfortable doing that. It was the dollar signs that were signalling in her brain. She could have a beer. A cold beer on a night like this would be nice.

Robyn moved further along the street to a bar that seemed not too busy but had the sounds of a mix of jazz and soul drifting out onto the street. The worker on the door gave her a nod and waved her in, and as she entered she was hit by the smell of food. Spicy chicken, garlic and other spices, and that well-known smell of good old mashed potatoes and gravy.

Her stomach gave a low grumble as she headed to the bar and bought a bottle of cold beer. Conscious of the fact she didn't want to sit on one of the high bar stools, she made her way to the far wall and slid into one of the wooden booths. The lights were dimmer here, and it gave her a chance to study the menu and the prices.

She'd almost talked herself out of it when a figure slid into the opposite side of the booth.

She started, ready to tell the stranger she didn't want to share, but instead she was met with a wide grin of perfect white teeth, and a set of gorgeous green eyes. Avery slid another bottle of beer across the table to her.

'Where did you come from?'

He nodded backwards, 'I was at a table with some of the theatre technicians. I saw you come in.'

She looked around self-consciously, but couldn't see the people he was referring to. She glanced at the beer again, noticing it was the same as the one she was drinking.

He was wearing a white T-shirt and blue jeans. Perfectly casual with his dark hair looking more ruffled than usual. And as soon as he'd sat down, she got that little whiff of his aftershave. Or maybe it was just his anti-perspirant, or his washing powder. Whatever it was, she'd started to associate it with him. It was clean, fresh and strangely alluring.

'I only came in for one,' she said, knowing it sounded awkward. But Robyn was conscious of not really wanting to end up in a drinking circle and contributing to a bill she might not be able to afford.

'Well, have two.' He smiled. 'You'll need one to have with dinner.'

'I wasn't planning on having dinner.'

'Really?' He stared at the menu in front of her. 'I was going to recommend the spicy shredded chicken with the rosemary mashed potatoes.'

She'd been looking at that on the menu. Could this guy read her mind?

'You've had it before?'

He gave a sorry sigh. 'I've tried most of the things on the menu in here. This place isn't too far from my apartment, and let's just say I can get by in the kitchen, but am not exactly a connoisseur chef.'

She gave him an amused glance.

'Eggs,' he said quickly. 'I can definitely do eggs. But…' he held up his hands '…eggs aren't exactly dinner.'

He leaned across the table towards her. 'Go on. I don't want to eat alone. Let me buy you my favourite shredded chicken.'

It was the easy way he said those words. A wave of recognition swept over her. This was a guy that had never really needed to worry about money. She knew without thinking that he'd never needed to consider his bank balance before purchasing something. She knew he'd never stood in a store counting up the change in his pockets to see what he could actually afford.

He'd never talked about money in front of her. But Robyn had been at the opposite end of the poverty spectrum for too long. When she saw a patient, their financial position was one of the first things she considered. Dependent on what country she was in, did they have medical insurance? If she was back in Scotland, what kind of home did they live in? Was it damp? Did they eat regularly? Were they dressed properly? Poverty affected so many aspects of people's lives, with direct links to their health. While that was recognised everywhere now, at heart, not everyone considered it on every occasion. It was the reason she'd aced the programme application. They'd told her that. Few had been as thorough as she was, directly linking health inequalities to both ends of the financial spectrum.

They hadn't asked about her financial circumstances in the interview. She'd worn clothes from a charity shop in Glasgow in one of the wealthiest parts of the city. She knew she could fake it like the best of them. But nothing would change what ran through her veins. And she didn't want it to change.

Which was why her fingers twitched and she subconsciously pulled back her hands on the table. Away from Avery. It wasn't a deliberate act. It was as if her body had gone into protective mode.

'I have to go,' she murmured, just as her stomach growled loudly. It was as if her body gave up all its secrets around him. Sabotaging her.

'You can, as soon as you eat something.' He leaned back, putting space between them, to separate the fact they'd just looked much more intimate with each other than they really were.

'I know I can't tell you what to do. I have a female best friend. I know much better than to do that, and also that it's a battle I would lose anyway. And I certainly don't want you to feel unsafe in any way.' He took a deep breath. 'Robyn. You're a colleague. I hope at some point you'll call me a friend. You look tired. I know it's stressful coming to a new place. After all the arrest calls you dealt with recently, you must be running on adrenaline. Let me buy you dinner. No pressure at all. I get the feeling you've not had a chance to make friends in San Diego yet, and I want you to enjoy your experience of working here.'

As he spoke, his voice lyrical and calm, the tension started to dissolve out of her muscles. This must be how he did it with the patients. The easy manner, the relaxed and reasoned point of view.

He'd told her she couldn't leave until she'd eaten something. But the decision was hers. She knew that. And the shredded chicken had been exactly what she'd been looking at on the menu.

She couldn't remember feeling relaxed since she'd got to San Diego. She felt as if she hadn't had time to draw breath. Robyn closed her eyes for a few seconds. She'd come into this bar because she liked the atmosphere, the music and the scent of the food.

Did she really need to be so uptight all the time?

She opened her eyes. Avery was looking straight at her. She pressed her lips together for a moment then nodded. 'I'd love to try the shredded chicken,' she said.

Relief swept over his face, he waved to one of the nearby waitresses and gave their order, settling back on the cushions in the booth.

'When are you working this week?'

Robyn took a sip of her beer. 'I only have another two shifts. I came straight into twelve days in a row. It was an initiation of fire, but things seem to be more settled now.'

'I'm glad you came in here tonight,' he said. 'You know the chocolate you like?'

She was surprised he remembered and she nodded, slightly confused.

He broke into a wide smile. 'I'll show you a small store in the next street. It's one of the few places that doesn't sell UK chocolate at exorbitant prices. The guy that owns it has Scottish grandkids.'

'Really?'

He nodded. 'He comes from Aberdeen. When he talks, I can make out about one word in ten.'

Robyn laughed. She looked up as the waitress passed with loaded plates, heading to another table.

She groaned. 'The smell in here is just heavenly.'

Avery nodded. 'Agreed. Like I said, I come here all the time.'

Robyn bit her lip, wondering if she should ask the question that was playing on her mind. 'You live around here?'

'Yeah, I've got an apartment I used to share with Serena not far away. We shared during our training, and then afterwards for a short while.'

'Ah, this was the friend you mentioned before. The one who moved in with the love of her life? So, she's moved out?'

He nodded. 'Place sure is quiet now. And, of course, the dishwasher broke as soon as she left. Serena was methodical about the dishwasher, always loading and unloading it. Every time I touch it, the thing breaks. I swear it hates me.'

'You clearly don't pay it enough attention.'

'Don't you start.' He wagged his finger at her and rolled his eyes.

'Must be kind of expensive to live here,' Robyn said, her brain hoping she'd sounded casual. Maybe she could ask the hospital administrators about renting in this area?

'It's not too bad,' said Avery easily. 'There are much more popular parts of the city. We were lucky, we scored a place that actually has a view of the marina. It's not right on the marina,' he said quickly. 'But I can see it from the windows. It's a two-bath, two-bed apartment so we each had our own space. So, it worked out fine. I'll probably ask around in a while for another roommate.'

She gave a thoughtful nod. Of course, he would. And when he looked for a roommate, he wouldn't want one that would only be around for six months. He'd want someone who planned to stay. And she was clearly losing her mind since she had not a single clue how much an apartment would be to rent in San Diego on a monthly basis.

'Have you seen much of the city yet?'

She shook her head. 'Not with the working hours, but I'm hoping to get around in the next few days.'

'You need to try the old town trolley. They do a tour, and you head to the other side of the marina to Coronado. Get out there. The beach is gorgeous. There's a beautiful hotel, and, despite what some people say, it's not just a military base.'

'Sounds fantastic. I've seen the other side of the marina when I've been running in the morning, and been curious. Just haven't had the time yet.' She gave a sigh. 'And I imagine the view when the trolley crosses the bridge is amazing.'

'It totally is.' Avery breathed in. 'I love my city. Even when it's packed with avid fans and conferences.' He held out his hands. 'There's a whole host of tours comes around the Gaslamp district seven days a week, several times a day. But I like that people come here and visit.'

'It's my first time in the US,' she admitted. 'I was hoping for huge shopping malls and outlets to buy running clothes for five dollars, but what little I've seen looks like normal prices.' She could feel heat rushing to her cheeks and wondered if she sounded like some kind of cheapskate.

But Avery smiled. 'You've just not found the outlet malls yet. I can show you. All of my international friends stock up as soon as they get here. My favourite was my friend who wanted to take home not just the sneakers, but the boxes too, and was livid when he realised he'd need to buy around three extra suitcases just to get them home.'

Robyn laughed. 'Well, I'm only looking to replace the running clothes and trainers that I have. I'm not looking for a supply for the next five years.'

The waitress appeared and set down their loaded plates. The smell of the spicy shredded chicken and rosemary mashed potatoes was delicious. Robyn put her nose close to the plate and sucked in a breath before picking up her cutlery. Her first taste was pure comfort.

Avery was watching her. 'You like?'

She nodded and smiled.

'Thank goodness. Imagine I'd just recommended something you hated.'

She shook her head. 'I'd actually looked at the menu and considered it. I just wasn't sure I wanted to stay too long.'

'I can walk you back to the hospital, if you're worried?' he said automatically. She looked up straight into his green eyes and almost caught her breath. There was something strangely hypnotic about being in this place with him. The dimmed lights, the background noise. The food and beer aromas, and the way his arms were positioned on the table, framing his upper muscles and broad chest. He was like a regular movie star. And when he flashed those perfect white teeth? No wonder they called him Mr Sunshine.

She felt oddly self-conscious. Her hair was pulled back in a ponytail band and she'd pulled on a summer dress in dark green. There was nothing wrong with how she looked, but she wished she'd put on a bit more make-up and a darker shade of lipstick—just paid a bit more attention to her appearance. It was stupid to think like that because she was sure Avery didn't care. But all of a sudden *she* cared. And she was having a hard time acknowledging that she did.

Her first reaction to his offer was to automatically say no. But something was stopping her. It would be dark by the time they finished their meal, and although the walk back to the hospital was fairly well lit, she would welcome the company until she was more familiar with the area. But was that the only reason?

'Thanks.' She smiled at him, before she could contemplate things any longer.

'No problem,' he said easily. 'Is there anything else you'd like to see around San Diego in the next few days?'

Her brain wanted to make an excuse, tell him she didn't want to trouble him—she'd find her own way around. But something about this was nice. Was welcomed. She shook her head. 'The sightseeing trolley, Coronado, and the shopping outlet seems enough for now. But if I think of anything else, I'll let you know,' she joked as she continued to tuck into her chicken and mashed potatoes. 'What I really need to do is try and get some sleep. My room is driving me nuts. I swear I hear reversing delivery trucks as soon as I try and close my eyes.'

Avery paused for a moment and then took a visible breath. 'Why don't you move into the spare room at my apartment, Robyn? I swear to you it's quiet. There are no reversing trucks on the high floors.'

Robyn was stunned and wasn't quite sure what to say at first. All her brain could focus on at first was the thought of sleep.

She really needed to rethink her bank balance. The money she was earning as a doctor now was reasonable. The programme also covered some expenses. But Robyn couldn't rethink twenty-five years of constantly counting every penny, finding ways to cut costs, and always wondering when the next disaster would happen.

Two months ago, she'd funded a new boiler for her parents back in Scotland. They could never have afforded a replacement on their own and they'd need it for when the weather grew colder again. She'd likely need to help them over the winter with the rising heating costs too. Would she be able to do that if she rented a room in Avery's apartment?

'How about I show you around it and you can see what you think?' he asked.

Robyn automatically nodded. 'Sure, that would be great.'

That would also give her time to think. To sort out how much she could afford and think of everything she would say if it was out of her price range—she might actually just tell him the truth—or, if she wasn't sure about renting a room with someone she worked with. It might make things a little…odd.

'Want another beer?' Avery asked. He had a grin on his face. It was clear the invitation had been easy for him, whereas it was making her brain spin in circles.

Robyn shook her head. 'Two's plenty. I'm a bit of a lightweight when it comes to alcohol,'

she confessed. 'Even though I'm from Scotland and it apparently runs through our veins.'

'Should I report you?' he joked.

'Too late,' she said. 'I'm a lost cause.'

'I wouldn't say that.' His lips had curled into
a smile and the words hung in the air between
them. 'Come on, then. I'll show you my place.'

'Now?'

'Why not? It's not far from here. I've got a
spare room. It's furnished and has air conditioning. There's a bed in there. Seriously—' he
held up both hands '—nothing untoward, but if
you're honestly finding it that tough, and you
need proper sleep at night, you're welcome to
stay at mine.'

Robyn found it hard to answer. Partly, because her brain was going to other places. But
also because finally getting uninterrupted sleep
would be pure bliss. She'd honestly considered
finding a cheap hotel for the night just to get
some peace.

She licked her lips. She couldn't pretend she
wasn't attracted to Avery and would like to
live under his roof…preferably in his room,
with him. But that wasn't the offer. Was she
offended?

She took a final sip of her beer, clearing her
throat and smiling. 'I'd love to get some sleep.'

Voices in her head fought to be heard. How

much did she really know about Avery? She was prepared to consider living with him, but why was her first thought mild offence that there was no other implication to his offer than platonic friendship?

Because, deep down, she knew she would be entirely safe under his roof. Nothing would happen unless she invited it. No one at Paz Memorial had a bad word to say about this guy. And she understood that.

They walked out onto the street and she followed him as they threaded their way through the crowds.

'You might find that I sleep for a week,' she admitted as they crossed at a walkway.

He shook his head. 'You've only got two more shifts, then, if you need to catch up on some sleep, that's entirely fine. Sleep as long as you like.'

Her mood brightened. 'Air conditioning.' She sighed.

He nodded. 'Air conditioning. I might even stretch to some Scottish candy bars.' He raised his eyebrows.

He was joking, and she laughed, while her skin tingled.

'Promises, promises,' she said.

He took her into the entrance of a high-rise building. The lobby was plush. The elevator took them almost to the top floor, and when it opened there were only two doors.

She'd been looking online at apartments and usually there were four on each floor. But as soon as Avery opened the door to his place, Robyn knew it was bigger than the average apartment.

It had light wood floors, and white walls. But the focal point was the huge windows. On one side, they had a view of the city, on the other, she could see the marina. The kitchen and sitting room were open-plan. Again, the space was the thing that captured her attention. Avery pointed in one direction. 'Serena's room and bath were down there. Mine are at the other end of the hall.'

'Wow, you mentioned the views but I wasn't expecting this,' she said, walking over to the nearby floor-to-ceiling window and just breathing as she looked at the spectacular view of the marina. Sure, it wasn't right next to them, and there was another high-rise partially blocking the complete view, but it was still pretty special.

'They are nice.' He tilted his head to one side. 'Even if you have to squint to get the full view.' He was teasing again and she reached over and gave him a gentle shove.

'I'm surprised you haven't been deluged with

people from the hospital asking to stay here.' A tiny thread of dread started in her brain. Maybe the price was just too outrageous?

He gave a sigh and pressed his lips together. 'I haven't really told anyone I was looking for a roommate yet. But since Serena moved out, it's been quiet around here.' He held up one hand. 'Not that she was noisy. But sometimes it's nice to get in at night and have someone else to talk to.'

Her stomach gave a little lurch. She got that. Loneliness frequently echoed around Robyn. She knew at times it was of her own making—she'd found dating hard since her sting in medical school. Or maybe it wasn't the dating that was hard, but more the trusting that came alongside it. Robyn had been so keen to protect herself and her heart that she'd kind of shut herself off from any potential suitors. Maybe it was time to take a breath and rethink?

'Go and have a look about—see what you think,' said Avery.

She could sense an element of anxiety in his voice. Did he honestly think she wouldn't like this place? She didn't need to see another thing before saying yes. All she had to consider was the price.

She gave a nod of her head and padded down the hall and into a white-walled bedroom with a couple of bright prints on the wall. The bed was large and looked freshly made up. The door to the bathroom was open and it revealed white vanity units, a walk-in shower and toilet. The room she had at the hospital was less than half the size of the bedroom in here, and that included the tiny bathroom. This place was luxurious in comparison. The air conditioning was delightfully chilly. She could actually have sunk down into the delicious bed and wept.

She walked over to the window that looked out over the city. San Diego was a vibrant place, but this high up there was no noise. She pulled down the blind in preparation for a good night's sleep.

Her heart quickened in her chest as she walked back down to meet him. 'I love it,' she said without hesitation. Then, before she could think too hard, she asked the big question. 'How much?'

Avery hesitated. 'Actually…' His voice tailed off.

'Actually what?'

He pressed his lips together. 'How about we just split the utilities?'

She frowned and held out her hands. 'But what about the actual rent?'

He shook his head. 'I've got some special

circumstances here. Without going into details, let's just say I don't have to pay actual rent.'

Her frown deepened. 'Is this a friend's place? A relatives? Are you just house-sitting?'

'Something like that,' he replied non-committally.

She didn't want to pry further when he clearly didn't want to talk about it. 'How much are the utilities?'

He gave a number she could easily manage. She sighed in relief and walked back over to the window. 'This is for real, isn't it? You aren't just fooling me into thinking I'm actually going to be able to sleep?'

He smiled. 'I'm not fooling you. You can move in tonight if you want.'

Robyn moved over next to him and touched his forearm. Her mood had never been brighter. 'In that case, better get your muscles out. I'm going to need some help heaving my stuff over here.'

His eyes twinkled. He looked as happy as she was, and almost relieved, which was something she could think about later.

'Your wish is my command,' he said with a grin.

CHAPTER FOUR

THE LAST FEW days had been…strange. Avery was definitely avoiding Serena because she would be able to tell he was feeling antsy in a heartbeat and would grill him within an inch of his life. He wasn't sure he could take a Serena grilling right now, or what it might reveal.

Robyn had jumped at the chance to move in, and hadn't asked too many more questions about the rent. He hated the fact he hadn't been entirely truthful with her about who really owned the apartment. But he just wanted to get a better feel for how things were between them both, before he revealed a secret that could impact on his personal and professional life.

Sharing the apartment with her was…nice. More than nice, to be honest. He was conscious of the electricity in the air between them, but was determined not to act on it, and he really liked having her around. He loved her accent. It held his attention and pulled him in. He loved the way she dropped Scottish words into the conversation without thinking and he had to hold up a hand and ask her to back up and translate them. So far, he'd learned the meaning of crabbit, drookit, aye and fankle. He planned to use all of these words at some point over the next few days.

He wanted her to be comfortable in his place. And she had been. That first morning, he'd actually had to go and knock her up in the morning. That made him smile, and then groan, once he realised what Serena would say when he revealed that Robyn had moved into her old room.

Unfortunately, their scheduled time off had been cancelled after a number of colleagues all came down with a mystery virus, so the city tour had to wait a bit longer.

Extra hours working was making a lot of the staff look tired and be extra cranky. He was relieved they'd managed to get Robyn out of her hospital room in time to let her get some proper sleep. He'd spoken to the unit manager the other day, mentioning about nursing and medical staff working more hours than they should, and ensuring those were noted, and that everyone would get the time back once the rest of the sick staff returned to work.

Robyn had just finished with a patient when he heard her pager sound. She answered immediately and her forehead creased. 'I'm not quite sure what you're telling me. Is this a surgical patient?'

She took her notepad from her pocket and scribbled a few things. 'Yes, yes, of course, I'll come and see her. Wait? What? Has she coded?'

Within a few seconds, both Avery's and Robyn's pagers sounded. She didn't even wait for the message. 'It's the ER,' she said to Avery and started to sprint down the corridor.

He followed on her heels, wondering what on earth he was heading into.

It only took a few minutes to find out. Their patient was in the resus room and the staff looked slightly stunned. One of the surgical doctors was in the room. As soon as they came in, he spoke rapidly. 'This is Mabel Tucker, she's twenty-five and was one of Toby Renfro's patients. She had an open splenectomy around eight weeks ago after a road traffic accident and recovered well. She presented today with severe shortness of breath. Her oxygen sats are in the low eighties.'

Avery exchanged a glance with Robyn. 'Another PE?'

'Likely,' she replied. It was hard to believe

they'd been called down to a second patient in such a short time with the exact same condition.

These circumstances were different. Throwing off any kind of clot—including a pulmonary embolism—was a risk after the removal of a patient's spleen.

Avery looked at the monitor. Pulseless electrical activity. Not good. He knew exactly what this meant. If this twenty-five-year-old young lady had a pulmonary embolism it must be large and would likely be fatal.

He watched Robyn weighing the situation up. She did this in the blink of an eye. 'Get me the senior cardiac consultant on call,' she said to one of the ER nurses. 'Continue cardiac massage,' she said to the second.

The anaesthetist, Flo, ran through the door. She was a few minutes later than everyone else and had a small smear of blood on her upper scrubs. Robyn looked at her directly. 'Female, twenty-five, previous splenectomy, likely pulmonary embolism. Can you intubate for me, please?'

The anaesthetist drew in a breath and moved to the top of the table, getting to work. 'Let's do an echocardiogram and try and confirm this,' Robyn said as a healthcare support worker wheeled over the machine that was in the corner of the room.

'Avery, prepare me thrombolytics.'

He moved across the room, opening one of the emergency drug cupboards and locating what he needed.

Robyn stayed completely calm, pausing the cardiac massage for a few moments to allow Flo to complete her intubation, then again when she had the transducer in hand to perform the echocardiogram. Time meant everything right now. He knew that Robyn would direct the medicine to be administered rapidly. But rapidly for this drug meant over fifteen minutes. Cardiac massage would need to continue all that time.

'Is someone with Mabel?' he asked as he finished preparing the drug.

One of the ER staff nodded. 'I've put her husband in the relatives' room.'

Avery nodded, his gaze fixed on the screen of the echocardiogram machine as Robyn placed the transducer to look at the heart. There were several signs she could look for to try and confirm the presence of a pulmonary embolism, and it only took her a few moments to find one.

'Sixty by sixty sign, along with a dilated right ventricle,' she said clearly, turning to

Avery and holding out her hand for the medicine. Both were signs of a pulmonary embolism.

He saw a trickle of sweat run down her brow. She looked amazingly calm, but he could only imagine how she was actually feeling.

'Dr Shad is on today,' came a call from the doorway. 'He's on his way down.'

Avery moved over next to Robyn. 'I'll do this,' he said, connecting the drug to the cannula in Mabel's arm. 'Fifteen minutes?'

She nodded.

'You concentrate on everything else,' he said in a low voice. 'You're doing great.'

He saw it. The tiny flare of panic in her eyes. It vanished just as quickly as it had appeared. He wondered how some of the other doctors who'd started just before Robyn would have coped in this situation. All of them were capable and competent. But this? This was something else. He was pretty sure that at least a few of them would have panicked. A few might even have decided to call the arrest. Mabel's chance of survival was less than ten per cent. Nearly all of the people in this room likely knew that already.

He couldn't help but admire her calmness and tenacity. 'Can someone call up to Cardiac

Theatre on the fourth floor and tell them to ready the emergency theatre?' Robyn asked.

Avery kept his eyes flicking back to the large clock on the wall as he administered the medicine slowly. Another nurse had swapped in to take over the cardiac massage. It was amazing how quickly it tired out anyone performing the massage.

The surgical doctor who'd been there when they arrived appeared back at the door. 'I've let Toby Renfro know. He's currently in Theatre, closing as we speak.'

Robyn gave a nod. She signalled to the nurse performing cardiac massage. 'Let's give it a few seconds to see if anything's changed.'

It was unlikely. The medicine wouldn't go through the veins in the normal way. The blood supply around the body right now was entirely dependent on how well the staff member performed the cardiac massage. After a few moments Robyn shook her head. 'Continue,' she signalled to the nurse.

Avery could almost see the relief emanate from her as Dr Shad walked through the door. 'Report, Dr Callaghan,' he said in a precise but calm manner.

She did. Sticking to essential facts. Dr Shad gave a nod. 'How many minutes?' he asked

Avery, looking at the medicine Avery was currently administering.

'It's been ten so far,' he replied.

Dr Shad nodded thoughtfully. 'Halt,' he said clearly to the nurse performing massage. Silence fell across the room as all eyes went to the cardiac monitor. Nothing changed.

'Call upstairs. Let's do a pulmonary embolectomy and try and give this young woman a chance. Everyone, prepare.'

This was why Avery loved his job. The anaesthetist unplugged her equipment and put it at the head of the bed. One nurse climbed up on the bed, ready to carry on with cardiac massage on the transfer. Another was on the phone, giving instructions upstairs. Dr Shad signalled to Robyn. 'You and I will scrub as soon as we get upstairs.' He turned to the surgical doctor. 'Tell Dr Renfro to join us whenever he is free.'

As the cardiac monitor was placed at Mabel's side, Avery took a breath. 'Dr Shad, no one has had a chance to talk to Mabel's husband yet.'

Dr Shad nodded and walked around, taking over the medicine administration from Avery. 'Apologise to him on my behalf. Bring him up to the fourth floor, make sure someone is looking after him, then join us in Theatre.'

Avery nodded, sure that his expression was just as surprised as Robyn's was.

He didn't usually assist in Theatre—although he'd done a rotation in there and was capable. He didn't ask questions—just assumed that Theatre had the same sickness problems as everywhere else. Robyn was also looking a bit shell-shocked. While all doctors on their programme would learn and assist in Theatre, it was usually around three months into their rotations. Robyn was only weeks into her placement.

Avery took a breath as the trolley holding Mabel swept out of the room and straight into the nearest elevator. He knew there would be a team waiting for them already on the fourth floor.

Tom Tucker was rigid in the chair in the relatives' room. He jerked as Avery opened the door. Avery hated this part of his job, but knew it was absolutely essential. This man had already experienced the recent trauma of his wife being in a road traffic accident and needing the emergency removal of her ruptured spleen. Last thing he needed was more trauma.

Avery sat down next to him. 'Tom, I'm Avery Smith. I'm one of the nurses from the cardiac unit.' Tom sat a little straighter, obviously wondering why someone from the cardiac unit was talking to him.

'Mabel is very sick,' said Avery carefully.

'We think she has a clot in her lung. It's stopped the air getting to her lungs properly, and her heart has stopped beating.'

'I saw you,' said the man, his voice monotone, as if he were in shock. 'I saw you and a red-haired woman working on Mabel.'

Avery was cursing in his head. He knew exactly how this had happened. Someone hadn't actually escorted Tom to the family room, and instead had simply pointed him in the direction of it. It was possible to see what was happening in the resus rooms if the curtains and doors weren't shut—and they hadn't been in Mabel's case because it had literally been all hands on deck.

'The red-haired lady is Dr Robyn Callaghan. She's one of the best doctors I've ever worked with. She gave the very best care to Mabel.'

He waited a moment, letting his words sink in with Tom. 'We've given her some medicine to try and break up the clot, but so far that hasn't worked. Our doctor, Dr Shad, has taken her up to Theatre to try and remove the clot from her lung.' He was always careful with the words and terminology he used around relatives. The last thing they needed in a crisis situation was not being able to understand what they were being told.

'Dr Shad's not her doctor,' said Tom mechanically. 'Her doctor is Toby Renfro.'

Avery nodded. 'Dr Shad is her doctor now. A clot in a vein is generally dealt with by a cardiac or vascular specialist. Dr Renfro is a surgeon. But he knows of her condition and we're hoping he'll join Dr Shad in Theatre.'

Tom breathed deeply for a few moments, then his eyes turned to Avery. 'Am I going to see her again?'

Avery swallowed. He was always honest with patients and relatives unless there was a specific reason not to be. He could only continue to be honest now.

'I hope so, Tom, I really do. Her condition is very serious and the survival rate is small. All I can tell you is that she's in the right place and has the best people looking after her.' He waited a few moments then touched Tom's arm. 'I'm going to take you up to the fourth floor where the theatre and cardiac unit is. Would you like me to call someone for you so you're not waiting alone?'

Tom nodded. He handed his own phone to Avery. 'Stephen is Mabel's father. Can you tell him, please?'

Avery nodded, took the phone outside and found a quiet space. He knew he was breaking Stephen's heart as soon as he got him on the phone. Stephen immediately agreed to come to Paz Memorial and wait with his son-in-law.

Avery wanted to get upstairs as quickly as possible. He wanted to get into Theatre—something he rarely did. But Dr Shad had asked him to look after Tom first, so that was what he would do.

They took the elevator to the fourth floor, where Avery showed Tom to a comfortable waiting area and spoke to the other staff. They were well equipped to look after Tom, and Stephen when he arrived, so Avery was waved away.

He headed straight to the changing rooms, switched his scrubs and searched the board to double-check which theatre they'd been assigned. He headed into theatre five, where the nurse in charge gave him a nod from the theatre table. 'Scrub,' she said.

The theatre was extremely quiet. All eyes were on the machines around the theatre table. A nurse on occasion was still standing and doing massage when instructed. But even from his slightly blocked vantage point, Avery could hear the occasional ping from the cardiac monitor. It sounded as though Mabel's heart was trying to function. It just wasn't in any kind of rhythm.

When he finished scrubbing Avery held out

his arms for a theatre gown and sterile gloves. He moved around the table, finally getting a proper view. Dr Shad and Toby Renfro were working side by side, talking in low voices. A thin catheter had been threaded through one of Mabel's veins and there was an extremely large clot in her lungs. At this point they were concerned that the clot might disintegrate into smaller clots and do even more damage to her heart, brain and other vital organs.

Robyn was right alongside the two experts. Her hands weren't shaking and she was using a retractor to hold back a portion of Mabel's skin. The charge nurse, Belle, who was holding a retractor at the other side, nodded to Avery. 'Take over from me,' she said, letting his hands replace hers.

As soon as she stepped back, he saw Belle wobble. He kept his hands perfectly still but turned his head. 'Belle?'

She took backward steps until she was leaning against the theatre wall. It was clear it was propping her up as she snapped off a glove and pulled down her face mask. She was deathly pale, her neat pregnant belly just visible underneath her layers.

The anaesthetist pressed a buzzer near her. 'You should have said something,' she scolded.

Belle shook her head. 'I'll be fine. I've gone

from one surgery to another without stopping. I just need to eat something.' She gave Avery a weak smile. 'I was never so glad to see you.'

The door edged open and a cautious head peeked inside. 'Do you need something?'

It was one of the theatre orderlies. Avery didn't hesitate. 'Can you assist Belle out of here, make her sit down and feed her, please?'

Mack had previously worked in the army medical corps and was great at his job. Mack's eyes went over to the far wall and widened with shock. 'Done,' he said. He moved swiftly across the theatre, put an arm around Belle and practically carried her back out.

'Time check,' said Dr Shad.

'Thirty-one minutes,' said Flo, the anaesthetist, clearly.

The interrupted cardiac massage had been ongoing for a long time. They all knew it wasn't realistic to keep this up for an extended period.

'There!' said Toby to Dr Shad. 'We've got it.' The clot was clearly visible in the proximal pulmonary artery.

Avery kept watch as they spent the next few minutes using a variety of methods. Removal of some of the clot, with further direct use of thrombolytics to reduce the size of it. It was the most delicate of procedures. Avery found himself first holding his breath, then meeting the gaze of Robyn, directly across the table from them. Everything about this event today had been full on.

Even the procedure now was different from normal. The wound in Mabel's groin was much wider than normal, probably because her circulatory system was so shut down it had been hard to access the vein. Avery's back ached from leaning over the table, so he could imagine how awkward it had been for Belle, with her pregnant belly and fatigue.

Robyn's blue eyes were steady. But he was getting to know her a little better every day. He could see the hint of panic there. She hid things well.

But she shouldn't have to. Even though this was modern day, sexism was still rife in the health services. He met it by being a male nurse, instead of opting to be a medic. Robyn had the opposite issue. Women were not the weaker sex, but tell that to their male counterparts, who seemed to find it easier to gain promotion across all fields in medicine.

He smiled at her underneath his mask, knowing she probably couldn't tell. But moments later little crinkles appeared at the outer edges of her eyes. She was smiling back.

'Got it,' said Dr Shad, his hands seeming like the steadiest hands on the planet as the catheter was slowly withdrawn. All eyes went to the cardiac monitor, which seemed to spring into life. A few blips with gaps in between, followed by slow steady noise. Blip. Blip. Blip. Avery had never been so relieved in his life.

The theatre wasn't jubilant. Everyone knew how serious things still were for this young woman. There was also the added trauma of the prolonged cardiac massage, plus the chance of her brain being affected by the potential lack of oxygen circulating in her system. No one would know the truth of that until Mabel woke up.

Dr Shad was meticulous. He closed and stitched the wound, had a long conversation with Flo and Toby about immediate plans for Mabel. She would be moved to Cardiac Intensive Care and remain ventilated for the next few hours, with assessment from all three doctors in six hours' time.

Avery could see Robyn following every word. The appreciation of their attention to detail and patient care was evident in her eyes. Some senior physicians would leave all the follow-up care to their more junior colleagues. But Dr Shad had never been like that, and Avery knew Toby was exactly the same. He was a caring and meticulous surgeon. It was part of the reason he approved of his best friend loving him. They were a perfect match.

'Mabel's husband, Tom, and her father will be in the waiting room. Who would you like to speak to them, Dr Shad?'

Dr Shad answered straight away. 'I'll talk to them. I'll apologise for not talking to them beforehand and give them an overview of what's happened.' He glanced down at Mabel. 'The next few days will be crucial, as will the next month for Mabel. She's beaten the statistics today, and we'll have to do our best to ensure she continues to have the best chance of beating them.'

'I'll come with you,' said Toby. 'I know the family well. They may want an explanation from me too.'

Dr Shad nodded appreciatively and completed Mabel's wound, allowing Flo and the newly arrived team from Cardiac Intensive Care to take Mabel around and get her connected up to all the equipment that would be needed for her care.

As the rest of the team exited through the doors it was only Avery and Robyn that were left. He stripped off his surgical gown, gloves, mask and hat, taking a deep breath at the relief of some air around his skin.

Robyn did the same, stuffing her disposable

garb into a nearby disposal cart, and pulling her scrub top from her chest. She moved over and leant against the flat theatre wall. Avery knew she would get instant relief from the cool wall.

'Belle,' he said quickly. 'Give me two minutes until I check she's okay.' He looked around at the rest of the theatre. 'And I'm not normally in here. I'll need to check the procedure for preparing the theatre again.'

'No need,' came a voice from the door, as one of the regular theatre team came in. 'Leave it to me.'

'Are you sure?' asked Avery.

The guy put his hand on Avery's arm. 'Go and have a seat for five. Everyone's talking about what just happened in here.'

'Thanks,' said Avery and gestured with his head to Robyn. 'You coming with me?'

It seemed natural to ask her. They'd done everything else together, and if she was surprised she didn't say, but her lips gave a soft smile and she nodded. They washed their hands again and made their way along to the theatre staffroom.

Belle was sitting in a corner, surrounded by food. She held up her cup and a cookie as they walked in. Her colour was much better and she had her feet up on another chair.

'Mr Sunshine, I could have kissed you when you walked into that theatre today.'

Avery walked over and kissed the top of her head. 'Well, I'll kiss you instead. I'm just glad you're okay. You should have told someone you didn't feel well.'

She blew out a breath. 'I know. I felt a bit light-headed when we went in. But it was such an emergency and no one else was available. I got caught up in the adrenaline of it all. I didn't have time to run about and find someone else.'

He sat in the chair next to her, picked a cookie from the bag, then handed it to Robyn. 'How many weeks are you now? Twenty-eight, twenty-nine?'

Belle gave the broadest grin. 'I love how you always remember. Twenty-nine.'

'Maybe it's time to take a breath now and then.'

'Oh, don't worry. You set Mack on me. Have you any idea what he's like? He says if he'd known I'd gone in there, he would have come and hunted me out anyway. He'd already re-minded me to eat.'

Avery nodded approvingly. 'In that case, I'm glad I set Mack on you. He has your back. That's what you need.' Avery leaned forward. 'Seriously, I know everywhere is short right now. I can ask if I can stay and cover here today if you need to go home and rest.'

Belle gave a laugh and slapped his arm. 'Avery Smith, you hate Theatre!'

He shrugged. 'I know,' he admitted. 'But if you need cover, I'll do it.'

She shook her head. 'I have more staff coming on duty in an hour, and all the surgeries are covered for today. We should be fine. But I appreciate the offer.' Her gaze flicked to Robyn, before she added, 'Not everyone would make it.'

She nibbled at her cookie and then spoke to Robyn. 'And you had an initiation of fire today. I promise you, we're not usually like that. I run a very refined theatre in these parts,' she joked, 'even if my past star student didn't pick it for their permanent job.'

'Thank you,' said Robyn, and Avery looked at her in surprise. It was the first time he'd ever heard a shake in her voice.

'Let's go,' he said smoothly. 'I'm glad you're feeling better, Belle.'

He stood up and held the door open for Robyn, waiting until they were halfway along the corridor, then taking a quick look up and down. No one else was around. He opened the nearest door, touched Robyn's elbow and indicated to her to come inside.

If she was surprised, she didn't show it. In fact, she willingly stepped inside the linen and scrub closet then put her hands over her face.

Avery froze for half a second, then did what his instincts told him to do, and wrapped his arms around her.

She started to shake and he knew she was crying. But instead of trying to fill the silence with a whole lot of words, he just stayed there, holding her, and letting her cry.

One of his hands rubbed her back, just the way his own mother had done for him years ago.

After she stopped shaking he bent his head and whispered in her ear. 'What's wrong? You did great today.'

For a moment she said nothing. He just felt her breathe, the rise and fall of her chest next to his. Then she lifted her head. Her blue eyes were red-rimmed. Her eyes were glassy, smudged with eyeliner that had run. Her hair was escaping around her face, tiny pink spots on her pale cheeks. It was the most vulnerable he'd ever seen her. 'Did I?' she asked, her voice angry. 'Mabel could have died today. If I'd been left with her, she *would* have died. I should have been more decisive. I should have acted quicker.'

Avery put his hands on her shoulders and

pushed her back a little so he could see her entire face. 'You did act decisively. You did a cardiac echo in the middle of the resus room on a patient who'd arrested. You made the clinical decision she'd had a PE and took it from there.'

She shook her head. 'But I should have made the call quicker. By the time we got upstairs too much time had passed. What if Mabel is brain-damaged because we took too long to get the clot out of her lung?'

'You had an anaesthetist intubate on scene. Mabel had the best chance of oxygen circulating around her system. First line for a PE is always a clot-buster drug. Even at rapid delivery it should be fifteen minutes.'

He could still feel her body tremble beneath his palms. 'Thirty-one minutes,' she murmured.

He tightened his grip a little on her shoulders. 'Don't focus on that. We have a responsibility to time the start of any arrest.' He shook his head in bewilderment and smiled at her. 'Robyn, you did good. Dr Shad will tell you that. He was impressed by you, I could tell. Do you know how often a more junior doctor gets invited into emergency theatre? Never.'

'But everyone's off sick,' she said, throwing her hands up.

'He didn't know that,' Avery said. 'He asked

you to come up because he considered Mabel your patient, as well as his. I know this guy. He didn't invite you into his theatre lightly.'

'Really?' For the first time since they'd come in here, he could see a spark of hope in her eyes.

'Really,' he repeated. He took a deep breath. 'Robyn,' he said slowly. Then, before he even thought about it, he was tracing a finger across her brow, and then down her nose. Her head moved automatically, responding to his touch.

Her gaze connected with his. Neither of them spoke. But Robyn, almost in slow motion, rose onto her toes and wrapped her arms around his neck.

The first brush of lips was tentative. But that lasted mere milliseconds. The next touch was definite. Sure. Without a single doubt.

The length of her body was pressed against his. He could feel every curve. His hand ran down one side of her body, tracing the outline of her waist and hips. Her lips were soft, matching him in every way.

He inhaled deeply, sensing the remnants of that spicy perfume he'd first noticed on her. His mouth went from her lips to her neck and to her ears. Her hair tickled against his skin, her breathing quickening.

His body was reacting to hers, and he

stopped for a second, conscious of exactly where they were. She sensed his reaction, and took a deep breath, letting him rest his forehead against hers. She smiled up at him.

'Well, that came out of nowhere,' she said huskily.

'Not exactly.'

Her blue eyes seemed brighter. She leaned back, keeping her gaze locked on his, then stepped back completely. 'We have to go back along to the unit.'

He nodded, adjusting his scrubs, knowing he wouldn't be leaving this linen closet for the next few minutes. Robyn bit her bottom lip and reached behind him, grabbing a clean set of scrubs. 'I'm going to head to the locker room and shower,' she said. 'After the ER and Theatre, I think I need to freshen up.'

He gave her a nod and smile, particularly when her gaze lowered. 'See you in five?' she asked.

'Absolutely,' he said. Robyn laughed as she walked out of the door.

Avery leaned back against the scrub trolley. What on earth was he doing? He'd always had his own rules about dating colleagues. His family life was complicated enough without letting his work life get complicated too. He was

still standing there when there was a sharp rap
at the door, followed by a recognisable laugh.

'You decent?' It was Serena's voice.

He groaned. 'Would it make a difference if
I said no?'

'Not at all,' she said as she pushed the door
open and stood in the doorway, grinning. 'Toby
told me what happened and I came to find you.
No one knew where you were.'

He leaned his head back. He knew exactly
what was coming next. Serena had that gleam
in her eye—the one that appeared whenever
she was about to tease him relentlessly.

She put a hand on her hip. 'But then, by
some weird coincidence, I saw Robyn duck-
ing out of here and into the changing rooms,
and I thought—' she put her hand under her
chin '—wait a minute…'

'Stop,' he groaned again.

'Not a chance.' Serena's grin was broad. 'I
thought, wait—' she mocked shock '—could
my good friend Avery, possibly, by any chance,
be in a *linen closet* with the feisty red-headed
doc he's been lusting over?'

'I have not!'

She clicked her fingers and shook her head.
'Nope. Too quick. The man doth protest too
much.'

He narrowed his gaze. 'Isn't that supposed to be the lady?'

'Who cares?' she declared, throwing her hands in the air. 'Spill.'

'Absolutely not.'

She folded her arms and stood across the doorway. 'I'm patient,' she said steadily. 'I can stand here all day.' She patted her stomach, 'And you can't push past me because I'm a pregnant woman.'

'Stop being smug.' He pointed at her belly. 'And I don't want my godchild to hear you trying to bully me.'

Serena raised her eyebrows. 'What my child is hearing is their mom sorting out their single, sad uncle Avery and helping him find his happy ever after.'

Avery rolled his eyes. 'You were never this unbearable before you met Toby,' he joked.

She pointed to her face. 'What you mean is, I was never this happy. Now, don't try and distract me. Robyn had a very interesting look on her face when she left this linen closet. Want to tell me why?'

Avery was instantly interested. 'Why? What did she look like?'

He could tell Serena was contemplating carrying on with her teasing, but she gave a sigh and said, 'Happy.'

'She did?'

Serena gave a shrug. 'I don't know her well. But from where I was standing, Dr Grumpy looked pretty happy.'

Avery couldn't help but smile. He hadn't even had time to think about what had just happened between him and Robyn, but the very fact that Serena said that Robyn looked happy made his heart miss a few extra beats.

'She might have moved in,' he said quickly.

'What?' Serena's eyes widened. 'No way. Not even you move that quickly.'

He shook his head. 'It's only just happened, and it's not like that. She was having trouble sleeping in her room at the hospital. I offered her your old room in the apartment.'

Serena opened her mouth and then closed it again. He'd clearly taken her unawares. She held up one hand. 'But, but—'

'But nothing. We've only been roommates the last few days. Nothing else.'

He moved forward and spoke down to Serena's belly. 'Right, tot, tell your momma to get out my way. Uncle Avery has work to do.'

Serena reluctantly stood back. 'Romance work, or real work?' Clearly still a bit stunned by all this news.

Avery tapped the side of his nose. 'That's for me to know, and you to find out.'

He started down the corridor, heading towards the cardiac intensive care unit.

'You know I will,' came the amused voice after him.

Avery didn't turn around. He didn't want Serena to see exactly how wide his grin currently was. So, he just lifted his hand and waved, as he pushed through the doors to meet Robyn, just as he'd promised.

CHAPTER FIVE

ROBYN WAS BUZZING. Her skin and lips were on fire, her brain couldn't stop firing either. Now she was sleeping in a perfectly peaceful apartment, it wasn't noisy deliveries to the hospital kitchen that were keeping her awake.

Yesterday had been one of the best, and one of the worst moments in her personal and professional life. And the weirdest part was, how all those pieces intertwined.

The arrest call had been devastating. Robyn could admit to herself how absolutely overwhelmed with panic she'd actually felt. She'd looked at the young woman lying on the emergency trolley and imagined herself, and every one of her friends, being that person.

There had been a real element of luck involved yesterday. The pulmonary embolism diagnosis had been pure instinct. But she could have been wrong. And if she had been, she wasn't sure what might have happened—except the certainty that Mabel would have died.

Avery had been the calmest man on the planet. The few times he'd caught her gaze she could almost hear him whispering next to her. *You've got this.* His calm nature gave her confidence in her decision-making, and she was so glad he'd been there.

Dr Shad inviting her into his theatre was, for any junior doctor, a dream come true. She'd had to will her hands not to shake, and her brain had tried to absorb every movement, every conversation, every technique she'd witnessed. She'd be processing this for days.

Then, there was the last part. The part that involved Avery Smith.

She was lying in her bed and just thinking about him made her skin prickle. The adrenaline had been running through her system so much at the time. She could remember the total exhaustion hitting her, plus the overwhelming emotions of the day, as she'd walked down that hospital corridor. Feeling Avery's arms around her had first been welcoming, then enticing.

She'd been conscious of the vibe between them—she just wasn't sure she was reading it correctly. Of course, he was handsome. Of course, he teased and flirted. He was nicknamed Mr Sunshine after all. There had been the looks. The atmosphere between them when they'd had dinner. His casual suggestion that he show her around the city. The offer of his spare room. And the building attraction between them now that they were under one roof.

But the one thing she was sure she'd read correctly was the connection between them and the kiss from yesterday. It had definitely been real. It had definitely been reciprocated. She hadn't flung herself at him. It had been a mutual meeting.

They'd both appeared back on the intensive cardiac unit. But all focus had had to be on Mabel and supporting her family. Robyn had had to stop her mind drifting back to the kiss and concentrate on the complicated regime of blood tests and drugs that Mabel would need for the rest of that day, and for the next few weeks. She'd been happy to stay late and take notes. Learning was why she was here.

It had been odd, watching the rise and fall of Mabel's chest following her ventilation, and watching it in conjunction with the beeping monitor proving Mabel's heart was functioning again. Of course, what she longed for was Mabel to be breathing on her own, and sitting up in bed, holding hands with her husband. But that could be weeks. Nothing could be taken for granted.

Nothing.

As they'd both finished last night Avery had hesitated next to her. Others had still been around. Some in earshot. So, he'd said very gently, 'I'll get us pizza on the way home.'

She'd been too surprised to give a response. But he'd just smiled and gone on his way. Home.

The word sent a little flicker of warmth through her body. She'd never really had great feelings of affection for her home with her parents. Their relationship had always been strained, and they'd never been all that interested in Robyn.

But back at the apartment with Avery? It was like living in another world. One where camaraderie existed. She was relaxed in a way she hadn't felt before.

They were both finally on days off for the next few days.

She couldn't remember ever being this muddled up by a guy. She dated. Or she didn't date. There was nothing in between. Never anything casual. It wasn't her style. But Avery didn't know her style—did he?

For the next few hours her brain continued to climb up mountains, then tumble down into valleys. It was ridiculous. She needed sleep.

But her brain wouldn't quieten enough to let her sleep.

Robyn groaned and sat up. She might as well go out. She glanced out of the window. It was a beautiful early morning in San Diego. She started most days with a run, but today her eyes were muggy and her muscles ached. She couldn't take pounding the sidewalks today.

Instead, she dressed in denim shorts and a white shirt, tied at her waist. As she grabbed her bag, a vision of cakes in a white box came into her mind.

Avery had been carrying a box when she'd bumped into him that other morning. She'd tried a few bakeries in the Gaslamp District, but there might be another she hadn't found yet. Hopefully it also sold the strongest kind of coffee. She could buy them breakfast before they went out this morning. That would be nice.

She stuck a clip in her crossbody bag for her hair in case she felt sticky, along with her wallet, sunglasses, sunscreen and phone. Some mascara and lipstick later, she walked out.

'Hey.'

She jumped. Avery was sitting on the sofa, dressed in jeans and a T-shirt and giving her his trademark smile.

She glanced at her watch. 'It's barely after seven.'

'I know. If you'd taken much longer I might have got cranky. I need coffee soon.'

'And if I'd decided to have a long lie-in?'

He grinned. 'I would have told you which coffee shop to meet me at, and you would have found me there, dehydrated, cranky, and probably shrivelled from all the heat outside.'

Robyn laughed out loud. 'Well, we can't have that. Makes you sound like a house plant I've forgotten to water.'

He gave her a fake shocked look. 'Are you a house-plant murderer?' He put a burr on his r's, attempting a Scottish accent, and Robyn kept laughing. He held out his hands. 'There's a reason I have no house plants.'

She wagged her finger. 'You're going to have to do better than that.' She looked out of the nearby window. 'It's going to be a hot one today, isn't it?'

'You bet,' he said. 'Let's just hope the air conditioning can cope.'

She closed her eyes for a second. 'Don't remind me what it's like to sleep in a room with no air conditioning.' She gave him a smile. 'I was going to go and get breakfast for us both.'

He gave a wide smile. 'Well, that's a nice way to start the day. But let's go together. What's it to be? Pastries? Doughnuts? Or eggs?

You need to tell me, so I can make sure we go to the best breakfast haunt.'

They left the apartment together and stepped into the elevator. 'Hmm, decisions, decisions… Isn't there a place that does all three?'

'Do you want all three mediocre? Or one out of three that's the best of the best?'

'Eggs,' she said quickly. 'Along with great coffee.'

They left the apartment and walked casually together. It was hotter than usual, and Robyn was already pulling her shirt from her body. He took her to a two-storey restaurant that looked over the marina.

It took coffee seriously. Robyn even got to pick the coffee beans she wanted ground from a huge selection behind the counter, as well as ordering a four-egg omelette with peppers, ham and cheese.

They settled at a table on the first floor, the windows folded completely back, in front of and behind them, to let the breeze flow through the entire restaurant.

Avery had pushed his sunglasses up on his head. The swim-trunks-clad model flashed into her head again and she tried not to smile.

'So, what's it to be?' he asked her.

'What do you mean?'

He pointed across the marina. 'We can do a

city tour on the trolley, cross the bridge, spend some time in Coronada, hit the outlet malls, or just wander around and watch the world. You gave me a whole list of things you wanted to do.'

'So, I can pick anything?'

He nodded. As their waiter appeared and set down her fragrant coffee and fluffy omelette, Robyn tried not to imagine this was going to be the perfect day. So far, it sounded that way. But she didn't want to put too much stake in things. It had been only one kiss, after all.

One heart-stopping, mind-bending kiss, so rational thinking was hard.

'Pick anything,' he reiterated.

She took a few forkfuls of her omelette. Perfect. Just the way it looked.

'Okay, so I would like to do all the tourist things and some more sightseeing. But I'd also really like to hit the outlet malls. I have a few things I need to pick up.'

'No problem,' he said with an easy smile. 'Outlet malls it is. There's one we can get a trolley to, and there's a stop not far from here. Looking to get some bargains?'

It was an innocent question, but Robyn automatically started coughing. She took a sip of her coffee and tried to form an appropriate response. 'I'd like some new running shoes to replace the ones I have. I don't need a particular design or label, just something that does the job. Same with running clothes and replacing a few staples from my wardrobe.'

He gave her a curious glance as he sipped his coffee. 'What, you don't want a particular type of designer coat, or bag, or computer? Usually when I take friends to the outlet malls, they want a whole host of designer gear.'

Robyn pressed her lips together for a second. Last thing she wanted was to sound like a misery-guts, or someone who was completely tight-fisted. She decided to go with the partial truth. 'I didn't have a lot growing up, so I don't spend money on things I don't need. I've always tended to wait until something was worn and needed replacing, rather than just splurge on things.'

'You never just buy something for fun?'

'Only in my dreams.'

He paused, before realising she wasn't joking. Robyn was aware of the strange silence between them and tried to fill it. 'My fun is books. I don't need designer bags or shoes or jewellery. If I treat myself, it's generally a book I really wanted and couldn't get in a library or online.'

Avery nodded slowly. He looked thoughtful for a moment. 'Not sure there's a bookstore at the outlet mall, but I'll be able to show you some when we get back. I might have a favourite I can introduce you to.'

The late summer heat in San Diego was rising around them, and Robyn felt a trickle of sweat sneak down her spine. She pulled her white shirt from her skin for a few moments, conscious of Avery's eyes on her.

'Want to go?' he said. 'There should be a trolley in a few minutes.'

She nodded and picked up her bag to pay the bill but Avery was too quick for her—not even asking the waitress, just moving over to the counter, handing over some dollar bills and coming back holding two bottles of iced water.

'I was going to pay,' she said.

'My treat.' His voice was insistent and she was uncomfortably conscious he'd paid for dinner the last time they'd been out too.

They walked to the trolley and Robyn bought her ticket from the machine—when she tried to buy Avery's he wouldn't let her. The trolley arrived quickly and was spacious enough for them to find a seat. It was busy, but not over-crowded, and the journey took around twenty minutes.

The outlet mall was a short walk from the trolley stop and Robyn smiled at the size of it. The buildings were spread out, bright, spacious, with many recognisable designer names across the store fronts.

'Do you need anything?' she asked as they started wandering through the outlet.

'I might pick up a few things,' he said casually.

Robyn got the distinct impression that while Avery didn't mind shopping, he'd only done this to keep her happy. 'Let's just stay here for a couple of hours,' she said quickly. 'How about around lunch time we head back and do some sightseeing?'

He gave a nod, and smiled when she pointed at one store and said, 'Let's try this one.'

It didn't take long for Robyn to find the few items she needed. She was a precise shopper—not the type to browse for hours or deliberate over things. She always knew what she was looking for, and if it wasn't there, then she just moved on.

As they left one store, and headed straight into another, Avery started to laugh at her.

'What?'

He waved his hand. 'I only wish all the females I know shopped like this.'

'What do you mean?'

'You waste no time. When I was a kid, my mother could spend hours in one place, trying on the same blouse in a dozen colours, trying

to decide what she liked best.' He pointed to a
set of benches outside the store front. 'I would
spend most of my time on one of those, generally with a soda or an ice cream.'

'Are you hinting?' she asked.

He looked confused for a second. 'For what?'

'Ice cream.'

'Ah.' He nodded. 'Probably, and I know just
the place.'

She walked alongside him. 'I've never been
someone who spends all day trying clothes or
shoes on. It's not that I never do that—of course
I do, if I'm not sure about a size or style. But
my friends back home used to call me the scanner.'

'The scanner?'

'Yes, they said I walked into a store, scanned
the whole place, spotted a few things I liked,
picked them up, tried them on and was ready
to leave by the time they'd reached the second
rail of clothing.' She gave a shrug. 'I think I
used to drive them nuts. They were much more
like your mother.'

Avery gave a smile. She could tell instantly
he was remembering something. He hadn't
mentioned his parents before. And she felt
compelled to ask the question.

'Is your mom not here any more?'

It should have felt more awkward and intrusive than it actually did. And Avery didn't seem upset or annoyed by the question. He gave a sad smile. 'No, not for a number of years.'

'I'm sorry,' she said simply. 'What about your dad?'

'He died fifteen years before my mom. They didn't have a great relationship—he was married to someone else when he met my mother and hadn't told her, so, although I knew him, I didn't get to spend much time with him.'

Robyn gave a nod.

'What about your parents?' he asked.

'They're fine,' she said, although that wasn't entirely true. 'They stay back in Scotland. Both have suffered some health issues.'

'They must love having a daughter that's a doctor, then.' She understood where he was coming from, but Avery had never met her parents, and probably wouldn't understand what they were like.

'I might have gone to medical school and worked across the world, but they don't ever ask, or take, my advice. They would rather listen to anyone else other than me. I can't seem to fight my way out of that "daughter" bubble.'

'You sound kind of sad about that.' Avery was looking at her curiously as they walked along.

'It's complicated,' she said, wondering how

much to reveal about her life. 'They don't live in the best area.' She lifted her hand in way of explanation. 'You'll understand that health inequalities are linked to deprivation. It's one big cycle that lots of people can't just break out of.'

Avery's brow creased and she kept going.

'You suffer from poor health that affects your mind or your body, and because of your poor health you struggle to get work. Then because you have no work, your income is reduced, and because your income is reduced you choose a cheaper diet and can't always pay the bills for heating—even when it's very cold.' She let out a big sigh, 'And then, because you're cold, that has an impact on your chest, lungs and the rest of your body. And the cycle just continues.'

Avery's steps had slowed. 'Is there anything I can help with?'

She froze and looked at him. Those green eyes were fixed on her, full of concern. She wasn't entirely sure what he meant. But she also knew she didn't want to find out.

Robyn was so used to playing her cards close to her chest when it came to her family. She'd always had a difficult relationship with her parents, and that made things tougher. She was passionate about the inequalities in health all across the world—that some people had access to healthcare and facilities, good housing and employment, while others didn't. With the most significant factor between the two parties being wealth. It made her want to sit in a corner and weep.

Trouble was, while most with a background in health agreed in principle, not all had the passion that she had. The courage of her convictions had resulted in many challenging conversations—particularly when a lot of doctors also came from privileged positions.

She chose her words carefully. 'I bought them a new boiler a couple of months ago, and I occasionally pay their heating bills for them. They're not always careful about how they spend money.' She gave Avery a cautious smile. 'But when I know that both my parents would rather spend money on cigarettes, and sometimes alcohol, than heating for their home or proper food, it causes a lot of strain between us.'

She could tell he was shocked. He tried to hide it, but Robyn was in tune with how people hid parts of themselves when these conversations started.

'Do you go home to see them often?'

She swallowed. 'Not frequently, and I don't stay with them if I visit. In truth, it doesn't really feel like home to me and it never really did.

But I try to help whenever I know there's an issue. To be fair to them, they don't normally ask. This time around my dad had a terrible chest infection that didn't seem to shift for a few weeks, and when I asked about the heating, my mother said the boiler had broken and couldn't be repaired. But if I hadn't asked that question?' She shook her head, 'I would never have known.'

Avery reached out and took her hand, entwining his fingers with hers. 'Families are tough,' he said. 'I know that. And our relationships with them can be even tougher. I won't comment, because it's not my place.' He gave her a stiff smile. 'And my pet hate in life is someone else commenting on a life they're not leading. The old *walk a mile in my shoes* thing, I'm a big believer in that.'

She looked at him with interest.

He tilted his head to the side. 'But later, if we have time, I'd like to take you to a place I work at.'

She gave a nod of her head. 'I'd like that.'

They'd reached the ice-cream store by now and looked in the window at the array of ice creams, sorbets and frozen yoghurts, and stood shoulder to shoulder. She contemplated his words, wondering exactly what she didn't know about Avery Smith. He'd never really spoken about his family before. Since they'd met, he'd struck her as a *found family* kind of guy. That was the general impression he gave around his relationship with best friend Serena. There were a few others that he'd mentioned, and she got the impression he would move mountains for his friends if he could.

She gave a little sigh as she looked at all the names on the ice creams. 'I hate that the world isn't fair. I hate that if you are born into money, a whole array of problems are just wiped out for you—whereas at the other end of the spectrum, if you're born into poverty, especially if you lose your job, or have an accident, it can send you into a spiral that there seems no way out of.'

'Lots of people who are rich have problems too. There's a million things that money can't buy.' He was looking at her cautiously.

'I know,' she said honestly, 'but it can also solve a whole host of issues that are insurmountable for others. I find that if people have money, they don't really understand the other side of the coin.'

There was an awkward kind of silence. She decided to break it. 'I'm just a sci-fi girl at heart. I want to live in the *Star Trek: The Next Generation* world where there's no need for money—where they've eliminated hunger, inequalities and the need for possessions.'

He raised an eyebrow. 'And yet Picard still managed to get into a whole heap of trouble.'

Robyn laughed out loud. 'Yes, he did,' she agreed. She pointed at the window. 'Okay, black raspberry and chocolate chunk is calling to me. What about you?'

His shoulders seemed to relax a little. 'Oh, I'm old school, chocolate mint with chocolate sprinkles.'

Robyn was thoughtful for a moment. 'Hmm, sprinkles, haven't had those in years. Okay, I'm persuaded.'

She had her wallet out before they'd even crossed the threshold of the store and paid for their ice creams before he could offer. 'Finished shopping?' he asked.

She nodded as she looked at her few bags. There were other people all around who were carrying so many bags they looked as though they might topple over. But even though she'd needed every item she'd purchased today, and they were cheaper than normal, she was still the tiniest bit uncomfortable having spent so much.

'I'm definitely done,' she said.

'Good, let's head back to the trolley, and we can join one of the tourist trams around San

Diego.' He looked up at the cloudless sky. 'It's a gorgeous day. If we go across the marina, you can see the beach at Coronado, and—' he gave a smile '—I've got an idea for something special this afternoon.'

Robyn gave a nod, and they walked back together. The slight tension between them seemed to ease, but she couldn't help but feel it had been her fault it was there in the first place. Avery was unfailingly easy mannered, but every now and then she saw a little flicker of something behind his eyes.

It was ironic really. She could talk. Her lifetime of pent-up frustrations of spending a childhood at the worst end of the poverty spectrum always threatened to bubble over. She was too passionate about things, had so many lived experiences that had, in turn, affected her life in a whole host of ways she hadn't fully understood until she was an adult. Some of it she was still processing today, and she knew at some point it would do her good to sit down with a therapist to take it all apart.

Most of the time she tried to keep things buried. She wasn't in that position any more. She would never be rich as a doctor—she would never do private practice and would likely return to the UK and work in the NHS—but she hoped to live above the poverty line in a way there had never been a chance to before. Doctors in the UK system weren't paid as well as people thought.

She didn't want to remember being hungry, or wearing shoes two sizes too small. She didn't want to remember not going to birthday parties of school friends because she could never take them a present—no matter how small.

Her library card had been her blessing. A place that was always warm, had electricity, and a world of information. She wanted to go back in time, and whisper in her own eight-year-old ear and tell her that one day she would be in America, she'd be a doctor, and be eating ice cream and visiting beautiful beaches and feeling the heat on her skin.

Her past self would never have believed it.

The journey back to San Diego seemed quicker and they boarded the orange trolley to take them around the city and over the marina.

As they travelled through the main parts of the city, Avery showed her the area where the free clinic he worked in was, and where the soup kitchen was. She knew just by looking that the trolley deliberately stayed away from the poorest parts of the city. She understood it, but it still made her sad. Why shouldn't people who visited San Diego see all of the city— the good parts and the bad? Then maybe they would have a more balanced opinion on how things were, and maybe even consider where they could help. Cities, worldwide, always had the richest and poorest of people, and she knew without doubt she wanted to help everyone, regardless of income or background.

'I'd like that.' She nodded and relaxed back into the trolley seat as it changed direction once again.

Robyn held her breath as they crossed the bridge. The view really was spectacular. The range of boats, from the military vessels to the luxury cruisers, was breathtaking. By the time they reached Coronado, the heat was building. Robyn rubbed on some sunscreen and handed it to Avery as they exited the trolley.

'Coronado means "the crown city",' said Avery as they started along the sidewalk.

Robyn looked around in awe. It was busy, with lots of holidaymakers, and a real vibrant vibe about the place. They wandered through the farmers' market, trying fresh berries, admiring the brightly coloured flowers available, and sampling a few cheeses.

The white sand beach stretched for two miles. There were ample sunbeds and parasols available for hire, families playing on the beach and in the sea. But as they moved further along, Robyn started to get excited.

'A dog beach?' she asked Avery, a wide smile on her face.

He nodded. 'Yep, there is a designated dog beach, where dogs can be let off the leash. Want to go down?'

'Try and stop me,' she said, moving swiftly onto the sand.

She couldn't help herself, asking owners if they minded, then stopping to talk to every friendly dog that she held her hand out to. There were terriers, chihuahuas, cocker spaniels, Great Danes, French bulldogs, retrievers, Labradors and whole host more.

'Didn't know you were a dog-lover,' remarked Avery, a look of pure amusement on his face. She noticed that more often than not he was down on his knees in the sand, letting dogs lick his hands and jump up on him.

'Oh, I never had one of my own. But I just loved them.'

'So, what would be your dream dog, then?' asked Avery.

'A fox red Labrador,' she said without hesitation. 'Friendly, good-natured dogs, but the red colour makes them just that little bit different.'

He was still grinning at her. 'Will you get one when you finish your training programme and decide to stay in one place?'

Robyn bit her bottom lip. 'The ultimate

dream? Well, it would be to find a for ever home that I could buy by myself—I don't care if it's tiny, as long as it's all mine, and yes, a dog to come home to.' She held up a hand. 'But my dog would need doggie day-care—and that would likely be as expensive as the house.'

Robyn bent down to pat another dog, who'd appeared at her ankles. 'I should have brought treats,' she murmured.

Avery shook his head as a huge Siberian husky bounded over and jumped up on him. 'Hello, girl,' he said without hesitation, not fazed at all by her jumping up, and rubbing her behind the ears.

'So sorry.' A woman rushed over and called her dog. 'Glenda, come back.' The dog's ears perked up and she ran back to her owner.

'No problem,' Avery said with a wave. He turned back to face Robyn.

'Glenda?' they both said at the same time, then burst out laughing.

Before she had time to think about it, Avery slung his arm around her shoulders. He looked down at her, and she instantly felt a rush. This didn't seem awkward. This felt like the most natural position in the world. 'You seem to have given this a lot of thought,' he said, still smiling.

For a few seconds she was lost. Lost in the

sensation of his body next to hers, and the scent of his skin. She couldn't remember ever feeling like this. Of course, she'd dated. But nothing important. Nothing that seemed significant, not even the guy at medical school. Not like this.

That final thought shook her out of her daydream. 'What?' she said as they started to walk along the beach together.

'The dog.' He grinned. 'You've given a lot of thought to getting a dog.'

She reached her hand up to clasp his hand that was on her shoulder. He was as close as he'd been all day, and she didn't want that to change.

'I have. I'm an adult now, and once I get my training programme finished and have a permanent post somewhere, it's definitely what I want to do.' She put her other hand on her heart as she looked across the beach. 'Imagine coming home to one of these wee faces. Someone that just loves you unconditionally. That is my idea of heaven.'

She was conscious of how the words sounded once she said them out loud. He couldn't possibly know she'd never had those feelings of love and security from her parents, and parts of her insides were cringing—praying that he didn't think she was actually hinting heavily about wanting a partner to love her unconditionally.

Well, of course she did. But right now, she was talking about a dog.

'It's the hours,' he said, and his words had a touch of melancholy to them.

'Yes.' She sighed in agreement, taking her free hand and sliding it around the back of his waist. 'It's the only thing that puts me off. Our hours can be crazy, and I couldn't stand the thought of my dog pining at home, wondering when I'd be back.'

'You should puppy share,' he said.

'What? What do you mean puppy share?' They were coming to the end of the leash-free beach and made their way back along the sidewalk.

'I have friends who puppy share. They both really wanted a dog. Did crazy hours, so decided to puppy share. They have some doggie day-care too, but it works well.'

Robyn stared up at him. 'Like some divorced couple sharing custody of a child?'

He gave a shrug. 'I don't know, maybe. But I can assure you, they're not a couple. Never have been, and both have their own places. They compare off-duty and holidays and try to do opposite shifts.'

Robyn started to smile. 'I've never heard of that. But it sounds great. Of course, it's years away, but it's something I'll think about later.

Thanks for that.' She looked at him, and he slowed his steps.

'No problem.' He bent down and kissed her on the lips as they were walking. It was casual, a momentary brush of lips. But it sent little pulses searing down her neck and chest. In her head she could see how they looked to other people—as if they had been doing this for years. But it wasn't. It was all brand new. And she wanted to savour it. To capture it somewhere so she could remember how this felt.

Her stomach gave a churn. It was like she already knew this would be taken away from her soon. As a rule, good things didn't really happen to Robyn Callaghan.

Her place on the programme had been due to her absolute hard work and constant studying. She'd sweated blood and tears for it.

But this? Nice things. Connections with people. They'd never really featured in Robyn's life, so she wanted to hold onto this with both hands.

And that made her scared. Very scared.

Last thing she wanted to do was act like some love-smitten teenager. If Avery acted like that with her, it would likely make her run for the hills. So, she couldn't quite get over the impact of feeling like that with him, and what she was supposed to do with it?

She could hear voices in her head from staff she'd met over the years. Kind folk, in a variety of hospitals, who'd realised how alone and isolated Robyn really was.

Just run with it. Take it a day at a time. Let things happen.

'I have another idea for doing something special this afternoon. Are you interested?' Avery's warm breath brushed against her cheek.

'Yes.'

'Are you ready to get the trolley back?'

'Absolutely.'

They boarded the trolley and she admired the view again as they crossed the bridge. It was a few stops before Avery signalled to her it was time to get off. He gave her a rueful smile. 'It's a bit of a walk from here.'

'No problem.'

He slid his hand into hers. She could tell they were moving away from the more prosperous parts of the city. The area they walked into was more run-down. Store fronts were closed, some vandalised. Housing was poorer, with broken shutters and roof tiles. The people around them glanced in their direction. If she hadn't been holding Avery's hand, she might have been nervous. But in a way, it was like walking back down some of the streets of Glasgow in the area in which she'd been raised. Her stomach twisted. She knew these people. She *was* one of these people.

Avery led her down the steps of a dilapidated-looking building with a nervous glance at her. He moved inside a cavernous space. It was like an old-style school cafeteria. Mismatched tables and chairs covered most of the space. They were filled by a whole variety of people who looked as if they were having a hard time in life.

At the other side of the hall a queue had formed.

'This is the soup kitchen.' She looked at him.

He nodded. 'It is. Are you okay that I brought you here?'

She squeezed his hand and smiled at him. 'Absolutely. How can I help?'

He should have known. He shouldn't have doubted that Robyn would roll up her hypothetical sleeves and get to work straight away.

She took to it like a proverbial duck to water and, after the few things she'd said today about deprivation and her relationship with her parents, his stomach was starting to churn with his secret keeping.

Robyn didn't hide her feelings about inequalities. She actively disliked the divide between rich and poor. She was entirely right. He agreed with her.

But that didn't mean he didn't come from a very rich family himself, or have inherited wealth. Even though he kept a low profile, and spent his time working at the soup kitchen, and the free clinic, he wasn't sure that would save him in Robyn's eyes.

The more time he spent with her, the more he liked her. He watched as she easily dished out food to some of the homeless that visited the shelter. She then moved among the clients, sitting and talking to them. She found a new coat for an elderly gentleman, a pair of shoes for another in the donation stacks that were held in the supply room. She even disappeared for a while with another member of staff to dress a young woman's wound that she'd acquired the night before, and wouldn't say where from. Robyn made her promise to return the next day to the free clinic for antibiotics.

Nothing seemed to faze her. He'd had the briefest moment of doubt before he'd brought her here. But it was all without merit.

'Sign me up for regular shifts here,' she said as she slid her hands around him from behind. He was standing in one of the back rooms, sorting through some donations.

He leaned back into her. 'Really?'

'Absolutely,' she said with conviction. 'I wish I'd visited earlier. I can work here during the rest of my time at Paz Memorial.'

He spun around to look at her, putting his arms around her waist. 'I love that you've said that.'

There was a gleam in her eyes. 'I'm curious,' she said. 'You told me you worked here, and at the free clinic. Did you know someone around here that made you want to do it?'

Avery tried not to gulp. He didn't want to lie to Robyn. He'd funded both the soup kitchen and the free clinic, but hardly anyone knew that and, considering her views, he didn't know how to tell her. 'I just wanted to give back,' he said, because it was truthful. 'When I worked as a student I saw a lot of homeless people coming into the ER. There had been a soup kitchen years ago, but it had closed due to lack of funding and volunteers. When this one started, I was one of the first to volunteer, and I've encouraged a lot of others from Paz Memorial to help out. But…' he glanced around '…more than fifty per cent of the volunteers here have nothing to do with the hospital. They've come because they want to. Some were even homeless themselves at some point.'

Robyn gave a slow nod. He could almost see

her brain ticking. 'It's a good thing to do,' she said, 'and I'm very happy to help.'

'Well, in case you weren't aware, you're fabulous.' He whispered the words in her ear.

'Thank you,' she said.

He moved closer, his voice low. 'May I?'

She answered by putting her hand on his cheek and meeting his lips with hers. His lips found their way to her neck and ears. Her hands wound their way through his hair and around the tops of his arms and across his back. 'Maybe we should head back to the apartment,' he said in a low voice.

She pulled apart. 'Maybe we should.' The twinkle in her eye was real. He knew exactly where this could lead.

He slid his hand into hers and led her back through the kitchen, talking to a few volunteers and clients before they left.

He was having a hard time concentrating. He bought pizza for them on the way home and some beers, before finally heading back up to the apartment.

Robyn wasted no time. She appeared a few moments later having changed into comfortable soft pyjamas and sat down on the sofa.

She patted the seat next to her and he put the pizza and beer on the low table in front of them, sliding his arm around her back.

'Good day?' he asked.

'The best,' she agreed, brushing her lips against his.

There was a flash in his head. She was only here for six months, and one month of that was already gone. He knew instantly that he couldn't continue to keep secrets from Robyn for another five months. Not when he knew the strength of her convictions.

Not when he knew how strongly he was coming to feel for her.

Maybe this would go someplace, and maybe it wouldn't. But the last thing he wanted to do was to destroy something before it ever really had a chance to grow.

He would tell her.

He would find a way in the next few days to tell her who he really was, to tell her about his family and why he kept things secret.

She slid her fingers through his hair and he groaned. 'I lost you for a second there,' she murmured.

'No,' he said quickly, turning his full attention onto the woman in his arms. The woman who seemed to fit there perfectly.

'You've got me completely,' he said as his lips met hers once again.

CHAPTER SIX

AVERY HAD SPENT most of the next hours of the early morning thinking how, and when, he could tell Robyn the truth about himself. He had checked on her before he'd gone for a run this morning, and he couldn't fathom the tickling feeling in his stomach at watching her sleep, her red hair spread over his white pillows. It had made him run harder, and for longer, as he'd rationalised everything in his head.

By the time he arrived back, the apartment seemed strangely silent. For the briefest of seconds, he thought she might have found out everything, and left.

Then he heard the shower running, and pretended the panic hadn't existed, and casually loaded a pod into the coffee maker.

When Robyn padded back down the hall with her hair all piled up on her head and wearing a pink T-shirt and denim shorts again, he had the oddest sensation.

Serena and he had apartment-shared throughout their training and afterwards. They'd been comfortable around each other, good friends and completely at home with each other.

This felt entirely different. Something he'd never, ever experienced before.

Those simple steps, and the smile edging around her lips, along with her still-sleepy eyes sent a message direct to his heart.

He wanted her to stay longer than five months.

It almost took the wind from his sails.

The rational part of his brain tried to tell him off. He didn't really know her. They'd worked together for only a short period of time. She didn't know everything about him.

But somehow, the message from his brain didn't get to his feet. Instead, they crossed the apartment and then he was kissing her.

Robyn threw back her head and laughed, before wrapping her hands around his neck and pressing her body up against his.

He walked her backwards. Back into the room they'd fallen into last night. He traced a finger down her nose. 'You sure?'

She gave him a grin. 'Oh, I'm sure,' and she rolled on top of him, and made him forget all about the conversations they needed to have.

* * *

When they finally emerged from his bedroom, Robyn disappeared for a while, coming back holding a stack of books. 'Do you mind?' she asked, gesturing to a half-empty shelf.

He gestured to a shelf that held a similar stack of his own. 'Help yourself.' It reminded him that they'd barely moved in together before they'd moved this relationship on.

'Sorry about the lack of sleep last night,' he murmured.

Robyn moved over and put her books on the shelf, raising her eyebrows at him. She sat back down next to him and smiled. 'We need to chat about rules.'

He set down the tablet he'd been holding. 'Sounds ominous.'

'I might have to restock your cupboards.'

'Phew, I thought you might say I can't disturb your sleep.' He gave her a suspicious look. 'What's wrong with my cupboards?'

She gave a casual shrug. 'I'm a girl of tradition. There's no pasta. No pasta sauce. No emergency frozen pizza. No jam. And definitely no emergency stash of chocolate.'

'Jam?'

'You call it jelly—but that's something else entirely in Scotland. I like raspberry jam on my toast in the morning.'

'You eat frozen pizza? I can make you pizza.'

She shook her head. 'Believe me. As a girl who has been a medical student for years, then a junior doctor, I have bizarre eating habits. You don't want me waking you up at three in the morning because I have a craving for pizza. That's why I need a few frozen.'

He gave a slow nod. 'And emergency chocolate.'

Robyn sighed and held up her hands. 'There *always* has to be emergency chocolate.'

'You're kind of bossy, aren't you?'

For a second she looked worried. 'I try not to be. But if I put my cards on the table, we'll get along better, won't we?'

He leaned forward and touched her arm. 'You think we won't get along?' He was grinning at her, and it only took a second before her pale blue eyes had a gleam in them.

She leaned forward too, brushing her lips against his. 'I think we might get along very well,' she said in a low voice.

He sank his hand into her dark red hair, pulling it free from its band and sending it tumbling around her shoulders. Her hair was always pulled back, neat and tidy at her work— just the way it should be. But loose around her shoulders, it was incredible.

'I hope you never get this cut,' he murmured.

'You like it.' The gleam in her eye had turned wicked. She brushed a strand of her hair across his face.

'Okay,' he groaned. 'Chocolate, pizza, whatever you want.'

She leaned forward and kissed him and then stopped. 'What is this?' she whispered.

'I'm not sure,' he answered honestly. 'I just know I've never done this before.'

She touched him with her hair again. 'You've never done this?' she teased sceptically.

He took her hand and sat it on his chest above his heart. 'I've never done *this*,' he corrected. 'I just know it feels right. And I want to do it. I want to see what happens next.'

'So do I,' she breathed, trying to stop tears from forming in her eyes. 'This connection terrifies me.'

He got it. He really did. 'Let's agree to be terrified together, then.' He smiled.

He was being honest. But he hadn't been totally honest, had he? And he would need to be with her. Part of Robyn struck him as raw—vulnerable even. He wanted to tread carefully with her. They were having this conversation. They were telling each other how they felt. But there was still a whole host of history, or background, of related trauma, of experiences, that every adult brought with them to any relationship.

They had time. They had time to learn about each other together. He didn't advertise parts of his life. He never had. Serena had found out by mistake, but, after the initial surprise, she'd been able to shake off any preconceived ideas. Serena had trained in San Diego, so she'd understood a little of his history. Would a girl from Scotland understand too?

He hoped so. Because he wanted this to mean something. To be worth it. Because he thought Robyn Callaghan was worth it.

There was something just beneath her surface. A vulnerability that she didn't wear on her sleeve—instead it seemed like armour around her heart.

He wanted to shield her. Protect her. None of which was his business to do. He knew it. He had to let Robyn be whoever she wanted to be.

He just hoped they could be something together.

He stood up and held his hand out to her. 'I get the feeling you're not going to help my sleeping pattern,' she said as she slid into his arms again.

'Nights are for sleeping,' he said. 'Daytime? That can be for something else.'

And she grinned and agreed.

* * *

They spent the next few days in their own little bubble.

They had a few beers in local bars, sampled coffee from the best coffee shops and restocked the kitchen to Robyn's standard. She introduced Avery to an orange fizzy Scottish drink, to several chocolate biscuits and mallows he'd never seen before, and lamented loudly the fact no other country sold Scottish square sausage.

Avery wasn't entirely sure he ever wanted to taste it, but smiled and nodded willingly.

On their last day off work together he took her to the place he thought she might love best. The store was tucked away down a thin lane, between two buildings. Not really an official avenue or street. Nonetheless, there was a number of quirky little stores.

The front facing was old painted wood. The sign said, carefully painted, The Book Emporium. It didn't have the traditional wide storefront glass window, instead it was like lots of tiny windows surrounded by white wood—a bit like a chess board.

As Avery pushed open the main door there was a tinkle above them, and Robyn smiled at the metal chime. 'Haven't seen one of these in years.'

He watched as she stepped inside and stopped. She was a book person. He got that.

Robyn breathed in deeply. The smell of books. The thing that some people thought they could replicate in a candle, and absolutely couldn't.

The expression on her face said everything. He'd called this right.

Robyn's eyes were bright as she looked around in wonder. The wonky shelves were labelled, and all different sizes. It was as though someone had bought bookcases from all around the world and hadn't cared about the dimensions. The range of books went from ancient and falling apart, to brand new. She was wearing a bright pink dress today that reached her knees, and her hair was falling around her shoulders. The only concession to the heat outside was a dark green headscarf she'd used to keep her hair from falling onto her face, tying it like a headband and making her look like a modern-day Alice in Wonderland.

A small lady with a tiny dog under her arm appeared from a cupboard near the back. 'Avery.' She smiled. 'Oh.' Her eyes widened. 'You brought a friend.'

He nodded. 'Hi, Annie, this is Robyn—we work together. I thought I would introduce her to the best bookstore in San Diego.'

Annie, with tight curly hair and dressed in a bright pink and green kaftan, set down her small dog, who promptly came over to sniff Robyn. She bent down to pat it. 'What kind of dog is it?'

'No idea,' said Annie easily. 'She won't tell me.'

Robyn caught Avery's gaze. She gave him a careful smile—a secret message that she understood. 'Well, I like her very much.' The dog had hair similar to Annie's—in fact, they weren't that different.

Annie gave her an approving glance. 'That's Peggy. If she doesn't like you, you'll soon find out.'

Robyn gave a calm nod and kept petting Peggy. 'Books are everywhere,' said Annie casually, with a throwaway action of her arms. 'If you need something in particular, let me know.' She wandered off back among the shelves.

Robyn's eyes twinkled and she grinned at Avery as she ran her hand along one of the shelves. She was only just noticing how far back this store went. 'How long have we got?'

'All day,' he said easily. 'There are tables and armchairs near the back if you want to take a better look at some of the books. And a word of warning—Annie sometimes refuses to sell.'

'A bookseller who won't sell?'

He nodded. 'She's very particular. If she thinks a book isn't for you—she'll tell you.'

Robyn glanced over her shoulder to the disappearing form of Annie and gave a little smile. 'Next you'll be telling me she's a witch.'

Avery's eyebrows shot up and he wiggled his hand in a 'maybe' gesture. Robyn sighed and started to walk among the stacks.

Avery settled down in a chair next to books on shipwrecks, military history and ancient Egypt. There was always something new to find here. He'd found an old medical book once that showed a very inaccurate circulatory system, and he'd kept a hold of it, to remember how far medicine had come.

Robyn flitted from section to section, collecting a pile of books on a table nearby. Some romance. A historical non-fiction book. A science fiction. The latest thriller. Then he heard a squeal of excitement and got to his feet.

'What is it?'

She was kneeling on the floor in front of a shelf of children's books, holding one in her hand. It was clearly second-hand, and part of a children's series from years ago.

The whole children's section was beautifully decorated. One of the shelves had a wooden castle outlined in lightweight wood attached to the front of it and clearly hand-painted.

One half was pink and purple with remnants of long-detached glitter, and the other half was grey and red with a green dragon billowing fire from one of the windows.

It was a little fantasy world tucked away in the corner of the bookstore to allow young imaginations to go wild. Instead, it had caught an adult, who was young at heart. He loved the fact she'd had no qualms about sitting on the floor and wrinkling her dress to find the book that she wanted.

'Do you know how long I've looked for this?' she said, clutching the book in both hands. 'I loved this series as a kid, but over the years I think my mum gave them all away. I've tried to get them back, with these original covers, and I've never been able to get this one.' She held it close to her chest. 'I can't believe I've finally found it. It must be at least thirty years old. My copy was already second-hand when I had it.'

He looked forward at the dark blue cover with a red lighthouse and two younger kids—a boy and a girl—standing in front of it. He'd had these books as a child too, but had never really fallen in love with the series. His mother had donated them to the local library. A thought probably best kept to himself right now.

'Is that the only one you need?' he asked.

She nodded. 'Some of the ones I've got are

really dog-eared. This one is actually okay, especially when you think how old it is.' She stroked the cover and smiled. 'I wonder how many people have read this copy?'

'I wonder how many have loved it as much as you do.' There was something so wonderful about this. The expression on her face at finding something she'd looked for.

The door swung open and the chimes rang out. 'Perfect timing,' said Avery and made his way over to the door. A delivery driver had arrived with steaming coffees and a large white box. 'Annie,' he called over his shoulder.

Annie appeared out of nowhere, bustling forward as if she'd always been there. She gave Robyn a knowing grin. 'He always buys me coffee from that fancy place on the corner.' She picked up one of the coffees, and opened the white box, selecting a cupcake covered in rainbow sprinkles. Her eyes caught sight of the book in Robyn's hands. 'You like that series?'

Robyn nodded enthusiastically, 'I've been looking for this particular book for ten years.'

Annie gave her a curious stare. 'That's probably how long I've had this one in my store,' she said simply. She turned to the pile on the table. 'Also yours?' She thumbed through the selection.

'Yes,' said Robyn.

'You're missing something.' Annie looked thoughtful. 'Give me a minute.' She disappeared among some stacks, stopping to touch one book, before shaking her head and moving on to another. Avery could tell Robyn was intrigued. He'd seen Annie do this on numerous occasions with visiting customers. Whether she was just insightful, quirky, or had an actual gift, he had no idea. He just knew that he liked this woman and found her store inviting.

'Aha!' came the voice. Annie emerged from the stacks looking surprisingly out of breath, and her hair askew. She thumped a book down on top of Robyn's pile. 'The perfect book for you.' She tucked all the books under her arm and took them to the old-fashioned cash register.

'On me,' said Avery in Robyn's head but she shook her head firmly and put her hand on his.

'Absolutely not. Books are the one thing I love to buy, remember.' Annie gave an approving smile and rang up the purchases, putting the dollars in the register and directing them to the back of the store.

Robyn was a bit confused, but Avery whispered in her ear. 'She likes everyone to sit down with what they've bought—to make sure they like them. If for any reason you don't, Annie will swap the books for you.'

'Really?' She looked astonished.

'Really. That's why I ordered the coffee and cupcakes. I knew we would be here for a while.'

He carried the rest of the coffees to the back of the store and handed out the extras to people who were already reading. Robyn followed his lead and set out two cupcakes on their table, and then passed around the box with the rest.

The tables were all different. Some carved oak or mahogany, others pine, all accompanied by a variety of chairs. Robyn's was high-backed and covered in red velvet. Avery's was lower, more like a wingback armchair, and was in dark green slightly worn leather.

Robyn leaned over to examine the stack of books. 'I don't even know what the last book she picked for me was,' she said, before examining the cover and then reading the back. She let out a laugh.

'What is it?' Avery sat forward, naturally curious. From his experience, Annie always picked the perfect books for her customers.

'It's about witches,' Robyn whispered, her cheeks turning pink. 'A modern-day rags-to-riches story of a misplaced witch who falls in love with a secret billionaire.'

She looked happy but shook her head. 'She obviously saw that I'd picked a few romances and she must have heard my whispers earlier.'

Avery was frozen. He knew he was smiling. And he hoped it stayed in place while his guts churned over and over. He'd never told Annie anything about himself. They'd had a hundred casual conversations in the past. He'd been in here with Serena before—but he was sure Serena wouldn't have mentioned anything either.

How on earth could Annie know about him?

'Avery?' Robyn's brow wrinkled. 'What's wrong?' She pointed at the cupcakes. 'Wanna swap a strawberry one for a chocolate one?'

He gave himself a shake. 'The book sounds great. And I'll eat any cupcake.' He took a long sip of his coffee, hoping the caffeine would sort out the mess that was currently his brain.

'What did you get?' She leaned over to look at his book on shipwrecks in the Pacific, and a thriller he'd picked up. It was as easy as that. She wasn't concentrating on the topic of her book any more. He breathed a sigh of relief but his brain was still working overtime.

He knew this wasn't an ideal situation. He'd dated in the past without letting people know his real background. But none of those had been a serious relationship. He'd never invited someone to stay in his home before, while officially being involved with them. This was different. This should have a whole new set of rules. With honesty being first.

Trouble was, in the past he'd kept his family background secret because the name was synonymous with enormous wealth. When he'd been younger, he'd wondered if girls were only interested in him because of the name and bank balance. And he'd certainly met a few like that. But since he'd changed his name, taken up an unknown career and kept his head well out of the limelight, he hadn't let anyone know about his inherited wealth.

Robyn had already made her feelings clear on wealth, inequalities in health and all the associated impacts. At times she even seemed angry about those things. Avery knew he would need to approach this subject cautiously. He didn't want to spoil anything between them. Not when things appeared to be going so well.

'I'll read this after you,' she said, tapping the thriller. She leaned back in her chair and took a sip of her coffee. 'This is a great place,' she said happily. 'I could spend all day in here.'

She nodded behind her at a man with bags around his feet and books all over the table he was sitting at. 'It looks like some people do that.' She bent forward, whispering, 'Please tell me that he doesn't read all the books and put them back?'

Avery shook his head. 'Annie wouldn't even care if he did. But people generally only come back here after they've paid for their books. And she's serious about swapping them. If you start something, and don't like it you can bring it back.' He gave another smile as he remembered something. 'There was a kid a few years ago, bought one book, read it, then brought it back. I think he kept swapping them out and ended up reading the whole series.'

'Annie didn't mind?'

'She didn't mind. She knows how the family were fixed. That's just the kind of person she is.'

Robyn was thoughtful for a few moments. 'It's a wonderful philosophy. But how does she keep her business afloat?'

Avery looked around too. 'She has a gift. A gift for people. Tourists love her and spend money in here. The locals wouldn't go anywhere else. She's able to balance things.'

Robyn stared at the table, her eyes focused on her books for a bit. 'Wish I'd known her when I was a kid,' she said softly.

Avery took a moment. He knew this was an opportunity to tell her. But he wasn't sure he should take it. 'You had a tough time as a kid?' Even asking the question made his heart ache a little. His mother might have broken away from her family, but he knew that he'd still lived a life of privilege.

'Some parts of Glasgow weren't so nice. The community—the neighbours generally were. And lots of families were in the same situation that we were. But it's draining. It gets you down. Never having money means that every single thing you do has to be weighed up in your head. And even as an adult, it's difficult to unlearn that behaviour—I'm not even sure I want to.' She took a deep breath. 'I have a salary now and some savings. But it always feels like it could be snatched away with no notice. I often wonder where I'd be if I hadn't managed to get the exam results I needed.' She shuddered—she actually shuddered. And that simple act brought home a whole host of emotions to Avery.

'Do you have friends from school who still stay there?'

It was the wrong question to ask, because he could see the wave of sadness that immediately crept over her face. 'Some. Not really friends though. One girl from school still stays in my street. She had three children and works part-time in the bookies.'

'The bookies?'

'Bookmakers. The betting shop.'

'Ah.'

'She's happy with her life. There are some families that never want or try to get out of the cycle that they're in. It's not up to me to decide that they're wrong.'

'You just wanted something different for yourself.'

'Absolutely.' She said the word with conviction. She took in another deep breath, picked up her cupcake and peeled back the wrapper, nibbling at the edges.

'How do you feel about going back to work tomorrow?'

Robyn rolled her shoulders. 'I'm ready for it. I'm looking forward to it. These last few days off have been…' she seemed to search for the word as her eyes locked with his '…nice,' she finished.

'Nice?' Avery was fairly sure his eyebrows had just reached the ceiling.

She laughed, and it was a sound he loved to hear. 'Well, more than nice, but we're in a public place. Decorum is required.'

'Are you sure?'

She leaned her head on one hand and said the word again. 'Absolutely.' Then she laughed and changed position. 'How about some home-made pizza tonight—can we go and grab a few things to make it?'

Avery nodded as he cleared his table and deposited their rubbish in the trash, stacking the books in his arms. 'Sure, there's a place just around the corner. We can get everything we need there.'

She walked out by his side and he was conscious of Annie watching them. He gave her a casual wave, but she didn't respond as she normally did.

Instead, she gave him a careful glance, then turned back to her shelves.

CHAPTER SEVEN

IT SEEMED THAT the gossip pipeline in Paz Memorial worked very well.

'You've moved in with Avery?'

'When did that happen?'

'What's his place like?'

'How on earth did you manage to land Mr Sunshine—you're not exactly Miss Happy yourself, are you?'

The last comment was made by a particularly acerbic nurse who'd already decided she didn't like Robyn, and Robyn didn't much care. She deadpanned her. 'I guess I just knew exactly what he *did* want, then, didn't I?'

She turned on her heel and walked away before her cheeks flamed. This chatter had better die down. She had a job to do, and patients to treat. She didn't relish being part of the hospital grapevine. It wasn't something she was used to.

Rounds were busy. A colleague was sick again, so she was covering the cardiac ward, and Cardiac Intensive Care. And, of course, she wanted to see Mabel Tucker again.

As she pushed open the door to the unit she could see Tom, Mabel's husband, by her bedside. Mabel was sitting up in bed. The ventilator was gone, but she was still wearing an oxygen mask, and her colour was pale.

Other things hadn't changed. Mabel was still surrounded by machines, still connected to things that monitored her heart rate, blood pressure and oxygen levels. There were two IV stands and a syringe driver slowly feeding fluids and drugs into her system. Mabel wasn't out of the woods yet.

But Robyn was just happy to see her breathing for herself. She wondered if Toby or Dr Shad had explained to Mabel how lucky she was to be alive. But of course not. The last thing Mabel would be feeling right now was lucky. That was a conversation for far in the future.

Tom was holding a tablet up and talking in a low voice to Mabel. As she moved closer she could see it was a photo of a cottage somewhere. 'We could try staying here,' he was saying, 'Or I found one near a beach, or another at a lakeside. Something to look forward to,' he said as he swallowed slowly, and even though Robyn's first instinct was to tell them that would need to be months in the future, she realised that he needed something to look forward to, as much as Mabel.

'Sounds lovely,' she said as she held out her hand and introduced herself. Of course, Mabel would have no idea who she was. She'd hadn't been conscious the whole time that Robyn had worked on Mabel. But Tom had been. She saw the flash of recognition in his eyes.

He grasped her hand tightly and shook it firmly. 'Thank you,' he said. 'I wasn't sure if you were just an emergency room doctor.'

'It's confusing down there,' said Robyn reassuringly. She held out her hands. 'But I mainly work here, on the cardiac floor. I've been off the last few days, and wanted to check in and see how things were going.'

'Your voice.' Mabel was frowning.

Robyn nodded. 'I'm from Scotland. I've got quite a strong accent, I'm afraid.'

Mabel looked at her, almost accusingly. 'I remember it.'

Robyn paused and nodded slowly. 'I worked on you for quite a long time and I went with you to Theatre. My voice is pretty distinctive.'

She was being careful. Most patients remembered nothing from major cardiac events. But, occasionally, some did. Robyn had never been sure if they were true memories, or pieces of information they'd been given just patched together. But her first thought was that it must be quite disorientating.

She pulled up a chair and sat down at the bedside. 'How are you feeling, Mabel? It's so nice to see you.'

As she sat down she noticed Tom's hands had a slight tremor. 'It's nice to see you too, Tom.'

'Mabel's dad was asking after you. He'll be sorry he missed you.'

'I'll be back in, and around for the next few days, so I'll keep an eye out for him to say hello.'

She turned back to Mabel, noticing the slight hitch in her breathing and her extremely poor colour. She looked anaemic. Robyn made a note to check Mabel's blood results. The medicines Mabel had been given to break up the clot in her lungs, and to stop another forming, could cause bleeding in other areas of her body. It was something that medical staff had to keep a close eye on.

A thousand thoughts flashed through her brain. If they would stabilise Mabel's blood levels. If there would be lasting impacts on her health. If she would ever be able to go on and have a family. If she'd struggle to find life insurance now.

But in that blink of an eye, she pushed them all from her mind.

It was a miracle that Mabel was still here. Still breathing. Still fighting.

'Are you hoping to get some time away and recuperate somewhere when all this is over?' she asked them both.

Mabel wasn't enthused. 'I can't think about anything like that right now.'

Tom looked pained.

'But hopefully you'll start to feel a bit better each day. You've had a traumatic experience. It will take time, and maybe some counselling, before you get over this. When you feel ready, a break away might be nice for you both.' She kept her words light and open. 'Do you want me to explain anything today, or do you have any questions?'

Mabel shook her head. Robyn understood. Mabel really wasn't ready to process any of this. She'd gone from one disaster—the car accident with its repercussions—to another that had almost taken her life.

'I was supposed to be starting my grade-school job.'

Tears glistened in her eyes and Robyn reached over and squeezed her hand. 'And you will. When you're ready. Life's thrown you some hard challenges. You need to find something positive to focus on, one step at a time.'

Mabel blinked. 'Like what?'

Robyn nodded. 'So, I'm not you, but if I'd had something similar happen, I'd feel like you do. I'd want to eventually get back to my job. But I can't do that straight away. So, what can I do? Well, I can try and get out of bed with some help and sit up for a few hours to help my back and posture. I could look for a more comfortable cushion than the one that's currently on my sofa. I could ask my partner to get me the next book in a series that's out this week, that I've been looking forward to. Oh, and the chocolate shop around the corner has a chocolate of the week. I'd make sure someone got me one of those every week.'

She sat back. 'It's hard, and only part of these things are under my control. I need a bit of help from my friends.' She pointed at Tom, 'Or family. But at least I'd feel as if I'd got a little control back, and was making some choices that were mine.'

Mabel looked thoughtful for a few moments then gave a tiny, but definitely wicked, smile. 'Or I could guilt one of my friends into giving me their password for a streaming service that I haven't subscribed to yet, and has a new series I want to watch.'

Robyn held up her hand and Mabel gave her a weak high five. 'I think you're getting the hang of this.' She smiled.

As she stood up to leave she turned back. 'I'll be back around later. We can chat again then if you want to.'

Thank you, Tom mouthed silently at her.

Robyn's heart gave a little skip. After feeling under the microscope for her personal life this morning, it was good to do the job she should be doing, and just be a doctor.

Her day continued well. She spent some time on rounds with Dr Shad. She was learning a lot from this man. He was generous with his time and expertise. She then shadowed one of the specialist cardiac physiotherapists, to see how best they encouraged both breathing exercises and physical exercise in patients with cardiac failure. It was part of the process she'd never really had time to concentrate on, and she welcomed the chance.

She was walking back to the nurses' station when one of the support workers gave her a shout. 'I've got a patient asking for you.'

'You have?' Robyn couldn't think who that might be.

'A Mr Hal Delaney? He's been in and out of here three times in the last month.'

Robyn nodded and sighed. 'What room is he in this time?'

The support worker gave a wicked grin. 'Well, the super-duper room is being used by another private patient, so he's had to make do.'

'Make do where?'

She pointed. 'Second room from the bottom.'

Robyn made her way down the corridor just as Avery came out of another room with a worried expression on his face.

'Hey, what's up?'

'I've got a young guy with cardiomyopathy. He's getting rapidly worse, so I was just going to find someone.' His brow creased. 'Where are you headed?'

'You know that guy—the first one we met at the arrest? He's back in again. He's asked to see me.' She paused. 'Want me to put him off, and come and see your patient instead?'

Avery shook his head. 'No. I'm going to find Dr Shad. The young man's normal doctor is on maternity leave, but I think I'm going to get our expert to take a look.' He blinked, 'No offence.'

She smiled brightly. 'None taken. Let me know how it goes. I'll be interested to hear how Dr Shad handles things.'

He reached over and touched her arm. 'Listen, there's something I need to talk to you about later. Away from here.' He glanced over his shoulder. 'Somewhere quiet, where it's just you and me.'

'Are you okay?' She felt instant concern. This wasn't like Avery. He looked so serious.

He nodded, the serious expression not leaving his face. 'Tonight, we'll talk tonight,' he repeated.

She held his gaze for a few moments, wondering what on earth was wrong. Another member of staff came up behind them, so she straightened her green shirt and put a smile on her face. 'In the meantime, I'll go and talk to Mr Delaney, who likely hasn't been following instructions he's been given. Seems to be his formula.'

Avery disappeared down the corridor. He seemed a little off and she wasn't quite sure why. Maybe he was just worried about the young guy.

She pushed open the door to the private room and, sure enough, Hal Delaney was sitting on the bed, a cross expression on his face.

'Mr Delaney,' Robyn said, keeping her expression serious. 'You asked for me? What brings you into hospital this time?'

'Chest pain,' he said quickly.

She walked over to the bedside. 'Any chest pain right now?' She noticed he was on an infusion of glyceryl trinitrate. She unwound her stethoscope from her neck. 'Mind if I have a listen to your chest?'

He shook his head and breathed in and out as she listened at the front and back of his chest. As she was listening the door behind her opened. She caught sight of a pair of dark trousers and shiny shoes. But no white coat.

'We're in the middle of something,' she said without turning around.

'See, Hal, she's trying to throw me out again.' There was an edge to the voice and she knew before she lifted her head who it was.

'Mr Paz, you seem to make a habit of walking into rooms where patients are being examined.'

He gave a fake laugh.

'Can I help you with something?' Her voice could cut steel and she knew it.

Hal coughed. Another symptom. He shook his head. 'It's okay.' He waved his hand.

She wondered about unconscious coercion. Because Hal knew Mr Paz through business, did he feel obliged to let him stay? Or were they really close friends, and this behaviour was normal? Were they, perhaps, more than friends? Robyn had no idea what to think, but she knew she had a patient to look after.

'If you're fine with Mr Paz staying, then we need to have a chat about what I heard. There's a definite degree of heart failure.' She noted his blood pressure on the monitor and looked at the level of his infusion. 'We need to review some medicines for you. Let me check your ankles too.'

She pressed her fingertips gently into his ankles to see if they left a depression. They did. Another sign of cardiac failure.

She sat down next to the bed. Mr Paz cleared his throat but she ignored him. Didn't he like his doctors sitting down? She didn't care. She wanted to be on the same level as Hal when she spoke to him.

'Sometimes after a major cardiac event— like the cardiac arrest you had—a heart can go into a degree of heart failure. What we need to work out is—is this a temporary thing while your heart still recovers, or is this permanent, and needs to be managed? Have you had a chest X-ray since you came back in?'

He shook his head. 'They ordered one. It's later today.'

'I'll also order a cardiac echo so we can see the heart muscles, the valves and the flow of blood through the heart.'

She glanced sideways at Mr Paz, before connecting her gaze with Hal's. 'Any issues with your waterworks?'

It was a potentially embarrassing question,

but he'd allowed his friend to stay, and Robyn needed to ask.

'What?'

'Do you ever have trouble passing urine?'

'Er…no. Why?'

'Because one of the things I want to do is start you on a low-dose diuretic. It will make you pee more. So, I need to ask the question, because if you have kidney, bladder or prostate problems, we might need to insert a catheter.'

'I don't think you'll need to do that,' said Mr Paz, followed by a strained laugh.

'I might,' said Robyn matter-of-factly.

Mr Paz's face reddened. The man really didn't like anyone questioning him. 'No, you won't,' he said stiffly.

Robyn bristled. She wouldn't stand for the man in charge of the hospital she worked in, needlessly questioning her medical expertise in front of a patient in need of care. He'd better be prepared to show her his medical qualifications if he wanted to continue like this.

She tipped her head to the side and pasted a smile on her face. 'Perhaps you would like to step outside and discuss this further?'

'Wait!' Hal raised his hand and Robyn turned around to face him.

'Leo, leave my doctor alone. I like her. And you know I don't normally like doctors. I think if you don't step aside, our Scottish girl will leave you lying in a corner somewhere and I don't want you to feel obliged to fire her. So, leave her alone.'

By the time he'd finished talking he was breathless. Robyn checked his oxygen saturation monitor and detached an oxygen mask from the wall, switching the dial up to five litres and sliding it over his face.

'Don't worry,' she said smoothly. 'We'll get you sorted.'

He squeezed her arm. 'I asked my chef to make you something special. For you, and the rest of your colleagues.'

She gave him a smile. 'I'm going to get the nurse to come in with a new medication for you to take, and we'll get those other tests carried out.'

She gave Mr Paz the briefest of nods as she walked past him.

Somehow, she knew he was going to follow her out of the door.

'Dr Callaghan,' he said as she walked down the corridor. His voice was a bit nasally. She had the horrible temptation to either ignore him or ask if he wanted a referral to an ear, nose and throat specialist. But of course, she did neither, because she was an ultimate professional.

As she went to turn around Avery came back

out of the room he'd been in before, this time with Dr Shad. 'Robyn,' he started and then stopped.

Dr Shad looked up. 'Dr Callaghan.' He nodded in a friendly manner, then noticed Mr Paz in the background. 'Mr Paz, what can we do for you?'

'I want to talk to Dr Callaghan actually, but it might be better talking to you, Dr Shad. You are, after all, one of our experts.'

Robyn could see the immediate creases in Dr Shad's brow as he tried to make sense of the situation, but as she turned back to Mr Paz he had a curious look on his face. He was staring intently, but not at her. He was staring at Avery, and as she turned to look at Avery she realised that he, too, had a curious look on his face.

It was only for a second, because as soon as she'd finished her turn towards him, Dr Shad had stepped up to her shoulder. 'I am one of your experts, Mr Paz, but Dr Callaghan does an excellent job. Is there something you wish to discuss?'

She could almost feel the defensive vibes flowing from Dr Shad. This man had her back. Avery would too, but she sensed movement behind her, and realised with a sinking feeling that he'd headed back down the corridor. She had the oddest sensation of something important happening that she should have been able to put her finger on, but couldn't.

Leo Paz had started talking. Or rather, he'd started whining. He had such an unfortunate manner for a chief executive. She couldn't imagine that he won any favours with the rest of his board. Dr Shad cut him off abruptly and held up a hand.

'I will not, and cannot, discuss Mr Delaney's care with yourself without his permission.' He stepped around Mr Paz and pushed open Mr Delaney's door. 'If you will give me a moment,' he said over his shoulder, making it abundantly clear that Mr Paz shouldn't join them.

Obviously slighted, Mr Paz turned back to her. 'That man in the corridor, who was he?'

Her skin prickled. She knew exactly who he meant. But all her natural defences had kicked in. 'Dr Shad? I would have thought you already knew him.'

'Not him.' He waved his hand angrily. 'The other man, with the dark hair.'

He was describing Avery only as a man—not as a nurse, even though Avery had stood a few metres from him, clearly wearing a nurse's uniform. She found it curious that he hadn't actually identified him. Avery had worked here longer than her, but then, maybe Mr Paz didn't normally walk the corridors of his hospital.

'I don't know who you mean,' she said calmly.

'Yes, you do, he called you by your name.' Colour was building in Mr Paz's cheeks. There was no use keeping quiet. He could ask Dr Shad, and she was sure he wouldn't have picked up the vibe that she had.

'That was Avery Smith,' she said, with no further explanation.

Dr Shad opened the door behind them, with Mr Delaney's electronic chart in his hand. 'I've spoken to Mr Delaney. He's agreed we can discuss his case with you, and is very complimentary of the care provided by Dr Callaghan. I've looked over her findings, test requests and decisions today and agree with everything so far. Can I ask why you wish to discuss one of my doctors?'

Mr Paz had opened his mouth a few times, obviously trying to take over. But Dr Shad was a determined individual, and once his diatribe had started, there was no way he was stopping.

'I... I wanted a second opinion on my friend's care. I thought he should be seen by a more senior and experienced physician.'

'Are you unhappy with the way I run the cardiac training programme, Mr Paz?'

There was a confused moment of silence. Dr Shad continued. 'Because if you are unhappy about the way I train those on the programme, I expect you to tell me.'

Mr Paz tried to gather himself. It was clear he'd wanted to start throwing his weight around but now regretted it.

'Dr Callaghan is an excellent physician and has provided some of the best emergency care. We are very lucky to have her in our service. She excelled in her previous studies—'

'She complained about a medical student.' Mr Paz cut Dr Shad off. Her skin prickled. Something had changed. She'd wondered if he'd been trying to catch her out before. Complain about her care, or her manner, but now? This had changed tack. Now, he seemed determined to pick fault with her, personally. Why was that?

She remembered the rude medical student, who apparently hadn't changed since she'd encountered him. Lia had told her he was related to Mr Paz, but since she hadn't heard anything else about it, she'd put it out of her mind.

'I complained about a medical student,' she conceded, before looking Mr Paz in the eye, 'because he was rude, overconfident, and lacking in clinical skills. He has some learning to do, and, because this is a teaching hospital, it's my duty to give feedback on those who require more supervision.'

Colour flooded into Mr Paz's face. 'Frank is an excellent student, and he will be an excellent doctor,' he exclaimed, clearly annoyed.

Robyn didn't flinch. He didn't intimidate her. Being brought up in one of the most deprived areas of her city meant that she'd been exposed to a lot, and knew exactly how to stand up for herself. 'Frank...' she used the name with purpose '...still has a lot to learn.' She gestured to the door. 'Would you allow him to care for your friend Hal?'

She felt Dr Shad's hand gently grip her white-coated arm.

'Mr Paz, I suggest we talk later,' Dr Shad said smoothly. 'Dr Callaghan and I have tests to arrange for Hal, and have to review his care. Once my clinical duties are completed, I will come and find you to discuss this further.'

Robyn found herself being turned around and guided back down the corridor and into a side office.

As soon as the door closed she didn't wait to be invited to talk. 'He's ridiculous. And I—' she put her hand on her chest '—was very reserved.'

Dr Shad gave a gentle laugh. 'You were, and I agree. He was ridiculous. But I didn't want to get into things with him right there.

His nephew is just about to have his placement revoked.'

'No?' Robyn was truly shocked. Medical students frequently did things wrong, it was part of the learning. She'd known of a few who had quit in the past—when they'd realised being a doctor wasn't for them. But she'd rarely heard of anyone having a learning placement revoked. It was the ultimate no-no.

She shook her head. 'What on earth has he done?'

'Exactly what you witnessed before. Talked dismissively to female staff, discharged patients without the authority to do so, and been arrogant, rude and disrespectful. I'd suggest that his learning ability is not where it should be.'

'I'm shocked,' she said dryly.

Dr Shad rolled his eyes. 'And I still have to tell Mr Paz about his nephew. Can you go and complete your work on Mr Delaney, and come back to me if there are any issues?'

She nodded her head. 'Of course.' There was a swell of pride in her chest. That Dr Shad had her back, and that he trusted her decision-making. San Diego had been a good choice for her. In more ways than one.

She continued her work and hurried down to the cafeteria to grab some lunch. She was late, so most of the good choices were gone. A coffee, a peach, and a sad-looking salad were what she took outside to the central courtyard. She could do with being surrounded by greenery for five minutes.

'Hey.' The voice behind her made her jump. Avery. For the first time since she'd known him, he didn't look great.

'You okay?' She wondered about earlier, but maybe he'd disappeared because he was sick.

He sighed and sat down opposite with a can of diet soda. He leaned his head on one hand. 'I need to tell you some things. But not here. It's not the place.'

A horrible feeling crept down her spine. 'Secret wife? Secret love child?'

He gave a half-smile. 'None of the above.'

'I've broken a rule in the apartment and you have to throw me out?'

'Not a chance.' He was almost smiling, but she could still see sadness in his eyes.

Her stomach somersaulted. 'Are you sick?'

He reached over and put his hand over hers. 'Not sick. It's nothing like that. But we need to have a chat. I don't want to do it here. I want to do it somewhere private. We can talk tonight.'

'You're worrying me.'

'I'm sorry. I don't mean to. I just need to tell you some things. I should have told you about them at the beginning.'

Robyn's head was spinning. She didn't know what to think. Was the happy little bubble she'd finally found about to burst?

Her page sounded to let her know that Hal's test results were ready. She stood up and gathered her rubbish, then bent forward and kissed him on the cheek.

And as she did so, she had a moment of realisation. She loved him. She really did.

She probably had for the last few weeks, but had been so busy guarding her heart that she hadn't let herself admit it.

But now, when there might be something wrong between them? It was like a spear in her heart. She didn't want to lose a love she'd just found. He said he wasn't sick, but that might just be an excuse. Her stomach squeezed. She couldn't bear the thought of Avery being ill. She really did love this guy. He'd captured her heart in a way that no one ever had.

Robyn had never had a connection with anyone else like this. Someone who genuinely respected her, and didn't try and change her mind about things. He accepted the way she was, how passionate she was about her job. The moment he'd taken her to the soup kitchen had cemented the place for him in her life. He got her. He really did.

'It will be fine,' she said, reaching over, cupping his cheek and looking into those green eyes and meaning every word.

She hurried back to the doors, taking one last look over her shoulder. Avery was staring at his hands. What on earth could he tell her that would make him feel like that?

Every cell in her body told her she really didn't want to know.

CHAPTER EIGHT

HE KNEW THIS day was just going to go from bad to worse. Some days were inevitable. And some were entirely of a person's own making. Just as his was today.

As soon as Leo Paz's eyes had set on him, he'd known his anonymity was over.

Maybe not instantly—but the flicker of confusion in his uncle's eyes was enough. Avery had always known working here was a risk. It was part of the reason he'd changed his surname to something he'd hoped would be forgettable. The surname Paz would have drawn attention to him straight away.

It was probably always inevitable he'd be exposed, but he'd hoped by the time people in the hospital had learned he was part of the Paz family dynasty he would already have proved himself a good nurse, a hard worker and a respectful colleague.

He still hoped that might happen. But right

now, he urgently needed to find the time to be straight with Robyn.

It seemed that Leo Paz had already fixated on her. Robyn had no idea what his uncle's wrath could be like. But Avery did. He'd witnessed as a child, first hand, what it had done to his mother.

To make matters worse—and it could only happen in the worst kind of story—it turned out the medical student that both Robyn and Avery had spoken to was also a member of the Paz family. From what Avery understood, that arrogant guy was likely to be his cousin.

He'd never met him before—couldn't have picked him out of a line-up if he'd been paid. But that was irrelevant. His mother had two brothers and two sisters. So, it had to be a child of one of his uncles or aunts.

This was why keeping secrets was never fun. He'd been blessed that Serena had never said anything. Though she had warned him this was a secret that would inevitably find its way out. And she'd been right.

His uncle usually never set foot on any of the wards, or in any of the departments. Avery could count on one hand how many times he'd seen him in the hospital during his nursing training and afterwards. Usually, it was whenever there was a new department opening and press was involved. Leo liked press attention, but these things had been easy for Avery to avoid.

His phone rang and he froze when he recognised the number. His family attorney. They only spoke on brief occasions, usually when Avery had to sign paperwork.

He was an older man, who'd been friends with Avery's mother and took care of all her family business on her behalf. Avery trusted him, and he knew Avery had trained as a nurse, changed his name, and worked at the Paz Memorial. There was only one reason he would call.

'Sam?'

'Avery, we need to talk.'

He sighed. 'Should I be worried?'

There was a long pause, then Sam finally said, 'I promised your mother I'd have your back. And I do.'

Avery Smith rarely got angry. No, Avery Smith never got angry. But Avery Paz? Oh, he definitely got angry.

He heard the shouting from the end of the corridor. This was a hospital, and someone was actually shouting.

He started jogging down the corridor. This couldn't possibly be good.

Robyn's voice was low, her accent so thick he could barely make out all the words. He knew she was talking but he couldn't hear properly because of the shouting by his least favourite medical student who was centimetres from her face.

The set of her jaw told him everything he needed to know.

'You think you can ruin me? You think you can badmouth me? I will destroy you! Who are you anyway? You think I can't find out who you are—where you come from? I won't just destroy you, I'll destroy your family too. I'm rich enough to do it!' Frank Paz was ranting.

Staff were coming out of rooms. Looking to see who was causing such a hullabaloo in their unit. But Avery got there first. Just in time to hear the reply from Robyn. 'This is your final warning. Step back from me and get a hold of yourself.' He heard her suck in a breath before she added icily, 'And if you threaten my family again, I'll break your legs. You stuck up piece of—'

Avery stepped between them, put his hands on his cousin's shoulders and pushed him back firmly. 'You heard the lady, back away and stop shouting, please. This is not the time, or the place.'

'You!' Frank seethed. 'You measly nurse.

What do you know? I'll ruin you too. Because of your complaining I'm getting my placement revoked. I'll speak to my uncle. I'll get this overturned and I'll get the two of you fired.' There was pure venom on the young man's face.

Avery's heart sank. He hated that he was related to a person like this. It reminded him exactly of why he didn't want to do what he was going to have to do.

Avery straightened his back. He easily towered a few inches over his younger cousin. 'How many times have you been reported to your supervisor?'

Frank blinked.

'How many times?' Avery repeated. He glanced over his shoulder to check Robyn was okay. She was clearly raging, but was catching her breath. 'Dr Callaghan reported you once, and I backed up her report because it was entirely true. A placement would rarely get revoked over one report. I can only imagine that there have been a multitude of reports about you for it to have reached this stage.'

He shook his head. He knew people were watching. At least he'd managed to stop his cousin shouting and disrupting the place. But everyone was waiting for what would come next.

'You, you're just a nurse. What do you know

about anything? This is nothing to do with you. I can get you sacked in a heartbeat,' Frank reiterated.

'Stop it. You're embarrassing yourself now. Take a look at your own behaviour. It seems that money can't buy good manners or a bit of humility.'

'Like you'd know.'

Avery bit his tongue. He could say something. He could wipe the smile off his cousin's face. But he wouldn't do that. It wasn't the kind of person that Avery was. And he wanted to have the conversation about his wealth with Robyn in private.

'He would, actually.'

It seemed fate had decided on a different path for Avery today.

He turned around to face his uncle.

'Avery Smith?' Leo Paz said with his eyebrows raised. 'Or Avery *Paz*? It seems that someone has changed their name. Now, that has to be a deliberate act. Why would you do that? So you could spy on how the hospital is being run?' He turned to face his other nephew. 'Your cousin here does know about money, Frank. He owns a fifth of this entire hospital. He could literally buy and sell you if he chose to.'

'I'm going to leave now,' Avery said calmly

to his uncle—even though he felt anything but calm. 'You can speak to my attorney.'

He turned to Robyn and held out his hand. 'Let's go.'

Her brow was wrinkled and she looked completely confused. 'What?'

Avery reached and took her hand, leading her down the corridor. He stopped briefly at the nurses' station. 'Can you let Dr Shad know we've had to leave?'

He put his hand at Robyn's back as they walked down the corridor. He could sense her breathing quickly. He wasn't quite sure where to start.

Her footsteps were slowing. He knew immediately they weren't going to get very far, so he steered them down the stairs and into the cafeteria, grabbing two coffees and taking them to the seating area outside.

He sat down opposite Robyn and she looked him clean in the eye. 'Explain.'

He breathed. At least she was giving him a chance to speak. 'Leo Paz is right. My name isn't Avery Smith. Leo was my mother's brother. He's my uncle.'

She blinked. 'And that rude medical student is your cousin?'

'He must be, but I've never met him before. My mother was estranged from most of the family, apart from her parents while they were alive. I think I met them all when I was a baby—but obviously I can't remember that. I've had no contact with any of these people in my memory.'

Robyn looked even more confused. 'So, Leanora Paz?' She held out her hands.

Avery nodded. 'The hospital is named after my grandmother. I don't remember her—or my grandfather either. He built the hospital as a memorial to her.'

'And you chose to come here of all places to work—why?'

He took a breath and wondered how on earth to explain this. He put his hand to his heart. 'Because it's in here. I have connections here that I've never been able to tell anyone about. My mother died here. I have huge memories of the time we spent in the cancer unit. As for the family? I know that some of them judged her way too harshly.'

He ran a hand through his hair. 'I've already told you my father was married to someone else when he met my mother, but she didn't know. I understand that my grandfather and grandmother were upset when she became pregnant, but they still loved her. They accepted me as their grandson. But her siblings weren't so forgiving or gracious and after my grandmother died they treated her very badly. She was estranged from them for most of my life, and she didn't want me exposed to their toxic behaviour. I've not been able to freely use the name I was born to. But this hospital is widely renowned. You know that. That's why you're here. And it's why I'm here too. I wanted to work in the best. I wanted to be part of something my mother's father created. And even though I couldn't tell anyone who I was, I wanted to honour my grandmother's name.'

Robyn's colour had steadily drained. 'Exactly how rich are you?'

Avery put his head in his hands. 'Don't do this, Robyn.'

'Why? I want to know. You've kept this from me. You've lied to me. You know how I feel about inequalities in health for people. You know I grew up with barely any money or chances. You can't even imagine what that's like.' Her hands were shaking.

'How much money do I have? I don't actually know—and no, I'm not lying to you. The apartment we're living in? I own the whole building. This hospital? Because I'm an only child, I inherited my mother's entire share. As Leo said, I own a fifth of this place. The free clinic I work at? I own that. The soup kitchen I help at? I own that too.'

Her eyes widened in horror and she shuddered. 'You own the whole apartment *building*?'

He nodded. 'The only people that knew who I was were my attorney, Sam—who was my mother's friend—and Serena.'

'Serena knows?'

He nodded. 'She found paperwork in the apartment when she was looking for something. She realised I'm part of the Paz family. But she's never asked me a lot of questions about it. She promised not to tell anyone else.'

'Your whole life is a lie.' Robyn spoke in a kind of far-off voice.

'Please, Robyn.' Avery leaned forward and took her hands, but she flinched and pulled them back. 'What happened between us wasn't a lie. I've never felt like this about anyone before. This is what I wanted to talk to you about. I wanted to be honest with you before, but it just never felt like the right time to bring it up. I might have been born into a wealthy family, but I try not to use the privilege it brings.'

'By buying an apartment block?'

He shook his head. 'It was my mother's. I inherited it. But I have bought things. I bought the clinic, and the shelter. I try to help people where I can. I work at the hospital under the radar. I don't want to rub my privilege in the

face of others. I try to live within my means.
I don't own expensive cars, and I don't wear
designer clothes.'

'But you still don't get it.' Robyn shook
her head. 'You can't. You don't know what it
feels like to go into a store and have to decide
whether to buy deodorant or tampons because
you can't afford both. You don't know what it
feels like to wear shoes that are so worn they
let in water constantly—or are too small but
you don't have enough for a bigger size. You
don't know what it feels like as a child to turn
down every party invite because you can't buy
a present.' She blinked back tears and he knew
just how strongly she felt about all this.

'I didn't choose the life I was born into,
Robyn. Just like you didn't choose yours. I try
to be responsible. I chose to train in a pro-
fession I know would have made my mother
proud. I work as much, and as often, as I can.'

She was shaking her head. 'But all those conversations we had—when we talked about elderly care. You mentioned the lack of provision
for them, and how poor care can be for the elderly. But you are sitting there with how much
in the bank?'

He leaned back and closed his eyes for a second. 'That's just it, Robyn. I can't help every
single person on this planet. No one would have

the finances for that. But I can help people locally. That's why I set up the free clinic and the soup kitchen. I pay the salaries and buy all the equipment needed. Take care of all the bills. I help where I can.'

She stared at him. 'But that must just scratch the surface.'

He nodded. 'I agree.'

Robyn stood up suddenly. 'I can't do this. I just can't. I can't be with someone who lied to me the way you have. Don't even dare try and say you didn't lie. Hiding the truth from me is the same as lying. And I can't get my head around this.'

'What?'

She pointed at him. 'You. You lied to me. You kept this from me. Did you think I wasn't good enough to know your secret? We've worked together closely for weeks. I moved into your place. We slept together! When would I have been trustworthy enough to tell? Or would that have been never?'

She started to shake. 'Everything between us has been a lie. Was how you even felt about me true—or was that all a lie too? Because how am I supposed to know for sure?' She started to pace, shaking her head as she spoke, and putting her hand on her chest as if it hurt. 'You know how I feel about this. You know how I feel about people being at opposite ends of the social spectrum. The privilege that comes with wealth and how it's all too often abused.'

She shuddered. 'How did I not see what was right before my eyes? You even look a bit like your uncle, and your cousin. I knew there was something off about Frank, and I just couldn't put my finger on it. It was the familiar traits. I can't believe I didn't see it before. I must be blind.'

She was ranting now and he didn't know how to stop her. He just wanted to make himself heard. To try and get a moment to tell her he was sorry, that he loved her.

'Look at the way they treat people,' she muttered. 'The entitlement. I can't do this. I just can't do this. I just can't be with someone with all that privilege.'

'You don't want to know me, be with me, just because I have money?'

He understood he hadn't been upfront with her, but he couldn't honestly believe that the fact he'd inherited money would mean that Robyn couldn't even consider having a relationship with him. She wasn't even giving him a chance to say anything else. The woman he loved was prepared to walk away from him for the simple reason that he had money.

She hesitated. And he could see it in her

eyes. For Robyn, that was true. Fundamentally, she didn't believe she could be happy with someone who was rich. It was as basic as that.

'I can give it away,' he said instantly. And he meant it.

His wealth had always played on his mind. It was why he'd kept his attorney to deal with so many things. He had foundations. He had scholarships in place to help underprivileged kids go to college or university. He signed the paperwork, but kept a distance from it all. He'd been conscious of staying under the rest of the family's radar. He didn't want to be involved in the family drama and infights that had caused his mother so much pain.

'It won't make a difference,' said Robyn sadly. 'You were born into wealth. You have a totally different outlook on life than I do. You can never really understand how things are.'

'Then teach me,' he said without a shadow of hesitation.

A tear ran down her cheek. 'I can't,' she said simply. 'I can't be that person for you. I don't want your pity. I don't want to be the poor girl, rescued by some rich guy.'

'I'm not trying to rescue you, Robyn. I'm trying to love you.' He put his hand on his heart. 'I've never felt like this before. I love you, Robyn. I don't want anyone else. I've never been happier since I met you. Please give us a chance.'

The tears were flowing freely now. 'I can't, Avery. Your uncle is probably going to fire me now, and throw me off this programme. Your cousin will likely get to continue as a medical student. Wealth and privilege can buy so much. I can't let myself be involved with you. I have to be true to myself, about my beliefs. I have to be able to look at myself in the mirror.'

'And you can't do that if you're with me?' He was starting to feel annoyed now.

She looked him straight in the eye. Her words were shaky. 'The way I feel right now? I don't think I can. I need some space. I can't be with you any more, Avery.'

She turned and walked out of the door.

He wanted to chase after her. He wanted to tell her to stop. To take her time. To give him another chance. But he knew she wasn't ready to do that.

His heart was breaking. But he also felt a flicker of anger and frustration that she refused to see him. The person she'd worked alongside, in the wards, in the soup kitchen. The person she'd lain next to in bed each night. She couldn't see that Avery any more. She could only see the dollar signs he represented. And it horrified him.

He took a deep breath.

His brain told himself to stay where he was. To let her walk away without going after her. To give her the space that she'd requested.

But when he got back home to his inevitably empty apartment a few hours later it still felt as if his heart had been ripped out of his chest.

He wasn't sure he would ever recover.

CHAPTER NINE

BETRAYED. THE WORD swam around in her brain and stayed there.

There was no other word she could use. He'd listened to her. He'd heard how hard she'd had things as a child. He knew she still budgeted— that she thought carefully about every single purchase.

And he'd still kept his billions secret from her.

Did he think she was in it for the money? Was that how Avery treated everyone he dated? It seemed odd to her he'd kept his wealth a secret from everyone.

She understood families argued and fell out. She understood families were estranged, and she could almost understand him wanting to work incognito at one of the most renowned hospitals in the US.

But she couldn't forgive him not telling her about the apartment block, or the free clinic, or the soup kitchen. He didn't just volunteer at the last two places. *He owned them.*

Packing up her things had literally taken minutes. Everything was thrown, crushed or crumpled into her cases and some shopping bags. She just wanted to get out of the apartment building as quick as she could.

It wasn't until she was back at the hospital in her tiny, noisy room that she realised something strange. The apartment block had a penthouse upstairs, and two much bigger apartments on the floor beneath Avery's. If he owned the place, why didn't he stay in one of those?

Was it all part of his ruse to keep his identity hidden?

The more she thought about it, the more confused she became. How had he managed to avoid his uncle Leo all these years? Her brain started putting pieces of the puzzle together. Now she realised why he'd disappeared that time in the ER the day they'd met. The same on the cardiac floor when Leo Paz had come to visit Hal Delaney.

His uncle was truly horrible. So was his cousin. Could she really blame him for wanting to keep his distance from people like that?

She sat on her bed, looking at her belongings. Everything bought and paid for by herself. She was proud of who she was, what she earned, how she managed her money, and still afforded to help her parents. She couldn't cope being swamped in money—and that was what life would be like with Avery.

It just wasn't for her. Even if he'd been truthful with her from the beginning, she wasn't sure she could have been with him. She could have kept his secret. But would her brain have got around how he managed to live with all that money in the bank?

She shuddered. She'd often thought, *How the other half live*. But Avery *was* the other half. He had wealth and privilege. He'd never known hunger, being cold, wearing clothes that were too small for him, or having to worry about paying for something.

She couldn't imagine spending her life with someone like that. How could he possibly understand the experiences she'd had? And while some people from deprived backgrounds might dream of finding a handsome billionaire, it had never, ever been something she'd wanted for herself.

Whenever she'd come into contact with those from a rich background, it had never gone well for her. The impact of that first rich boyfriend, who'd used her in medical school, treated her like a plaything—or, worse, someone to pity—had damaged her more than she'd ever admitted. Being dumped when someone richer and better connected had come along who could help him with his career had made her feel more useless than ever.

Had Avery felt like that about her? Hot, angry tears spilled down her cheeks and she couldn't stop the sobs. She'd told him more about her life than she'd told anyone before. The thought that he might actually have pitied her, felt sorry for her, made her feel physically sick with humiliation. The handsome man who'd made her heart flutter, who she'd actually thought was falling for her, the way she was falling for him, might only have been with her because he felt sorry for her?

She couldn't bear it. Not for a second. Who even was the genuine Avery Paz? She'd thought that she'd known him, thought they were connected. But now she could see she hadn't ever really scratched the surface. She'd only known what he'd let her know, and most of that was a lie.

She couldn't handle this. She wouldn't be made to feel like this. Used. Lied to. Worthless. She changed her clothes and walked up to the cardiac unit. Mr Paz was likely out for her blood now. If her career was about to be ruined because she'd dated his nephew, Robyn Callaghan wasn't going down without a fight.

* * *

Avery's phone rang again. His attorney. He answered. Sam didn't waste a single word. 'My office. Now.'

Avery made his way across the city. He considered changing his clothes, but what was the point? So he turned up at Sam's office in the wrinkled T-shirt and jeans he'd pulled on when he'd left the hospital.

Sam had a number of folders on his desk. 'Sit down,' he instructed.

Avery sighed and ran his fingers through his hair. His throat was dry and, as nice and loyal as Sam was, this was the last place he wanted to be right now.

His silver-haired attorney looked up. Sam was handsome. Some joked he was a Richard Gere lookalike, and Avery often wondered if there had ever been anything between Sam and his mother. At this point in life, he'd probably never know.

Sam turned around to a small glass-fronted refrigerator behind him—not too unusual in a hot city like San Diego. He pulled out a can of Avery's favourite soda and sat it in front of him. 'Buckle up.'

Avery blinked, surprised that Sam remembered, then popped the seal and took a drink.

'I always knew this day would come. I

warned you against working at Paz Memorial, but you were determined. It was inevitable that your uncle would discover you at some point, so we are prepared.'

'We are?' Avery was surprised.

'Of course.' Sam turned around a letter. 'I've been sent a number of requests from your uncle's attorney, the Paz family attorney, and the attorney of your aunt Marie.'

Avery shook his head. 'Why?'

'I can summarise. Your uncle wants to sue you for corruption, trespass, illegally spying on his business, gaining information by nefarious means, and a whole host of equally ridiculous things. He wants your share of the hospital and will try any means to get it. The Paz family attorney wants to know your intentions, and whether you intend to be involved in Paz Memorial, and if you want to assume your seat on the board. Your aunt wants to know if you will go and see her.'

Avery sat back, stunned.

Sam nodded. 'The list from your uncle is actually much larger. He also wants possession of the free clinic, and soup kitchen. Claims you have funded them by stealing equipment and—' he raised his eyebrows '—food from the hospital kitchen.'

Avery folded his arms. He was beginning to see where this was going. 'And the rest?'

Sam flicked through some files. 'Wants to sue you for your nursing licence, claiming malpractice, and dismiss you, and another person—a Ro—'

'Robyn Callaghan,' Avery cut in. He stood up. 'No. He can come for me all he wants. He can't go for her.'

Sam's eyebrows shot up. 'Who is she?'

Avery wasn't sure how to answer. His head was swimming. He'd spent the whole walk here still simmering with anger. Of course, he'd been wrong not to tell Robyn his secret. He should have told her as soon as he'd realised how he felt about her. But he was also annoyed that she hadn't stopped to take a breath, to see him, and not his money. He'd even wondered if maybe it was better she'd walked away, if she couldn't see past her prejudices and give him a chance. But now? No. No way. As soon as he knew his uncle was coming for Robyn, he was ready to go to war for her.

He could do this. He could see her again. He could give her the opportunity to cool down, and then sit down again together to discuss their relationship. That might all take time. But for right now? Avery would do everything he could to protect her. 'She's…she's someone…

I love. She's a great doctor and does incredible work. He can't touch her.'

Sam looked him in the eye. 'This is America. Dubious claims are made against doctors all the time.'

'They came for my mother before. She wanted me away from all this. This is the exact reason I've always kept away from my family. They won't go for Robyn. Tell my uncle I'll meet him tomorrow.'

Sam shook his head. 'Not a good idea.'

'I don't care.'

'You should. I promised your mother I'd look out for you.'

'Then look out for me. Come with me.'

Sam held his gaze for the longest time. 'I won't let you do anything foolish, Avery. You have that mad look in your eye.' He gave a sad smile. 'I recognise it. Your mother used to get it when people made her angry. It wasn't wise to stray into her path.'

'Then you'd better make sure the path is clear.'

Things weren't any better in the hospital. Robyn had barely taken a few steps into the unit before she was surrounded by staff.

'Is Avery really a member of the Paz family?'

'Is he a billionaire?'

'Why on earth is he working here if he's a billionaire?'

'Why did he even bother training as a nurse? He doesn't need to work for a living.'

'Did you know about this?'

'Yes, yes, I don't know, I don't know, and no. I had no idea,' Robyn answered as the questions were thrown at her.

A hand fixed on her arm. Serena, her eyes laced with worry. 'Where is he?'

Robyn stared at her. 'I don't know. I left the apartment. He's probably there.'

'I've already been there, and to the clinic and the soup kitchen. He's not at any of them.'

Robyn shook her head. 'I don't know, Serena, and right now, I don't care. He lied to me. He knew how I felt.'

'I don't imagine for a second that he lied to you,' she said quickly, her pregnant belly looking larger than the last time Robyn had seen her. 'He just didn't tell you. That's different. And he was going to tell you. He wanted to tell you.'

Robyn's skin bristled. He'd obviously talked about her to Serena. She didn't know if she liked that. Serena looked around at the still gossiping staff.

'You're not supposed to be working today, are you?'

Robyn shook her head.

'Then get out of here. You won't get a moment's peace. Take a walk. Go to the marina. Have a cocktail. Anything but hang around here.'

Robyn glanced around. People were staring at her. She and Avery were clearly the talk of the place. All of a sudden she felt swamped. Serena grabbed her arm again. 'Come on, I'll get you out of here.' She peeled Robyn's white coat from her shoulders and folded it over her arm, walking her to the stairwell, down the stairs and out to the main entrance. She stuck her hand in her pocket and handed over fifty dollars. 'You can pay me back later. Go and get some space.'

It was like living outside her own body. The last few hours seemed like a blur. As soon as Robyn walked out of the air-conditioned hospital and into the intense heat of the San Diego day, she knew she had to find somewhere cool, and away from spying eyes.

Her brain was whirling again. Had he outright lied to her? Maybe not, maybe he'd just answered questions carefully.

She'd thought earlier about seeing a counsellor about her past feelings. Now, she knew she needed to. Avery wasn't like her first boyfriend who'd let her down so badly, or like Frank and

Leo Paz. He didn't have the arrogance. Or the fickle outlook on life. She should have seen those things for herself. It really was time to unpick the damage her past had done to her. She had prejudices of her own that she needed to accept and deal with.

Her thoughts flicked back to the soup kitchen. The pride in Avery's eyes. And his interactions with the elderly patients in the ER. His patience and tactful care. This was the Avery she knew.

Her feet seemed to take charge. And before she knew it she was back in the Gaslamp district and pushing open the door to The Book Emporium with a jingle of the metal chimes announcing her arrival.

She didn't even glance at the shelves, just made her way to the back of the store and sat down in the same red velvet high-backed chair she'd sat in before. It took seconds before Annie's fluffy little dog started sniffing around her ankles and she picked it up and sat it in her lap. 'Hi, Peggy,' she murmured as she started to pet her. 'I think I need a hug.'

She jumped as a steaming cappuccino appeared in front of her, and, in a big whoosh, Annie sat down in the chair opposite. Her kaftan today was a mixture of yellows and oranges. There was absolutely no missing her.

She looked at Robyn curiously, but there was something else in her eyes. As if she knew everything already.

'What happened?' she asked.

Robyn didn't look up. She kept her eyes fixed on Peggy. It seemed safer. 'Oh, nothing,' she sighed. 'I found out the man I love is a secret billionaire, who chose not to tell me, even though he knew how I'd feel about it.'

'Why does his bank balance matter?'

Robyn looked up now. 'It matters because he didn't trust me enough to be honest with me.' She gave a little sigh. 'And I have issues. I grew up at the other end of that spectrum. I had a bad experience with a man once, and it's coloured how I feel about certain things.'

'Did you have a bad experience with Avery?'

'No…and yes. How do I even know if anything was real between us?'

Annie spoke quietly. 'Avery Smith is one of the nicest people I know. Kind, generous and handsome too.' She eyed Robyn carefully. 'He doesn't usually bring any girlfriends here. So, you must have meant something to him. What's not to like?'

'But that's just it. His name isn't Avery Smith. It's Avery Paz.' The words Annie was saying were pinging around her brain, falling into line with the thoughts she'd just been having on the way here.

'Ah.' Annie gave a knowing nod.

'You knew?'

'I guessed a long time ago. Avery looks very much like his mother, who used to bring him in here as a child.'

'But he never told me.'

'Because it probably wasn't appropriate. What if you were some kind of secret gold-digger?'

Robyn was horrified. 'I'm not!'

Annie shook her head and gave her a wry smile. 'Okay, you're not a gold-digger. Good. So, let's go back. What did you just say to me about Avery?'

Robyn creased her brow. 'I can't remember.'

'Well, I can. You said, *"the man I love"*.'

Robyn sat back in her chair as if someone had just knocked the wind out of her sails. It was ridiculous. She'd already realised that she loved Avery, but she'd never said the words out loud to someone else. 'We're not suited,' she said quietly.

'You're not suited because your brain won't allow you to be suited,' said Annie without hesitation. 'Why is it so insurmountable that you both grew up at either end of a financial spectrum? You can learn from each other.'

She looked away for a minute. 'You know that Avery works in the soup kitchen and free clinic.'

Robyn groaned. 'Avery *owns* the soup kitchen and free clinic.'

'Great.' Annie smiled. 'But Avery still needs to grow into his own skin. And you can help him do that. You can do that together.' She emphasised the final word.

Robyn shook her head. 'I don't think I can. It's just too much.'

Annie looked solemn. 'Avery has started so well. He's a Paz. And he's clearly been avoiding his family for good reason. But now, it's time for him to take back his name. You have to help him embrace that. He can do more good from the inside than he can from the outside.'

Robyn breathed. Trying to understand all of this.

'You have to decide,' said Annie. 'You have to decide how much you love him, and if he's worth the risk. Only you can do that.' She leaned over and lifted Peggy from Robyn's lap.

She started to walk away, then looked over her shoulder. 'And you should do it now.'

CHAPTER TEN

THEY'D JUST PULLED up outside the hospital in the car.

Avery was trying to get ready for this meeting. Sam's face was steely as they exited into the warm San Diego air.

'Avery!'

He recognised the shout before he even turned around. Robyn was running across the street towards him, her hair streaming behind her, and her eyes red-rimmed.

Before he even had a chance to acknowledge her, she had both her hands on his arms. 'What are you here to do?'

Sam shot a look at him. 'Robyn?' he asked.

She nodded and Sam took a second, taking in her unkempt appearance. Her shirt was half out of her trousers, her skin gleamed with sweat, and her hair was everywhere. He smiled. 'He's here to save your skin,' he said simply.

Robyn shook her head. 'Whatever it is you

think you need to do, you don't,' she said firmly. 'Your uncle is a bully. It's time you stood up to him. Don't do anything because of me. I can look after myself. I love you, Avery. I can be a doctor anywhere. But here? This is your place, your home. Take it back. Take it back from the people who made your mother's life hell.'

Her face was flushed, her beautiful blue eyes sparkling with love and warmth. Avery couldn't believe the sight in front of him. He ran his hand up the side of her cheek. 'Robyn Callaghan, I will not let my uncle come for you. I will not let him take from you what you've worked so hard for.' He held up his hand. 'I don't need any of this. I just need you.'

She wrapped her arms around his neck. 'You've got me, I promise. But fight, Avery. Don't give up anything that's rightfully yours. Be the person you should be. Be your own kind of Paz.'

His stomach clenched. She was right. He could do this. He could fight back against his uncle. And he would do it with Robyn by his side.

He held out his hand towards her. 'Are you ready to fight alongside me?'

She lifted her eyebrows. 'Was I born in Scotland?' She slid her hand into his. 'Let's do this.'

* * *

He'd finally put on a suit. He wanted to face his uncle on equal terms. Sam was by his side. And now, so was Robyn.

His uncle had three attorneys. None of whom were familiar to Avery.

Sam started by casually throwing a few papers across the desk. 'The ridiculous claims? Are just that—ridiculous. Threatening Avery's nurse registration, and the registration of his colleague, Dr Callaghan, is a low, cheap shot.' He looked Leo Paz in the eye. 'But, as Julia always warned me, not surprising.'

Avery jolted at his mother's name. Sam was clearly not prepared to play nice.

One of the other attorneys leaned forward and spoke a huge amount of legalese. It all sounded very impressive, but barely understandable. Avery picked up parts, from the sublime, to the ridiculous. Having to prove who he was. Objections to his mother's will that left everything to her only child. A list of all his assets that they had 'found' and now wondered how he had acquired them, and if they were actually family inheritance.

Sam was unperturbed, even though the man droned on for more than twenty minutes.

Eventually, Sam stood up.

'What are you doing?' Leo demanded.

Avery stood up too. 'We're leaving. There are more family members than yourself. You're not in full control here, and you seem unable and unwilling to talk. This is a waste of my time.'

Leo leaned forward. 'If you leave, I'll have your friend thrown off her training programme in the next hour and her visa to work here cancelled.'

Robyn moved first. She looked at Leo. 'Try it,' she said steadily. 'I believe Avery is entitled to a seat on your board. He'd like to take that up.'

Leo shook his head. 'You can't do that.'

Avery nodded to Sam. 'File the paperwork, Sam. I've some other things I need to do.'

He took hold of Robyn's hand and pulled her out of the conference room.

He looked her in the eye. 'You do realise what happens next, don't you?'

She gave him her steadiest smile. 'I stand by the man I love, fighting for what he knows is right.' She tipped her head to the side. 'I also need to move back into your apartment. Sort out my shifts at the soup kitchen and clinic.' She pressed her lips together for a second. 'Arrange to find a counsellor, and see if my time in the programme can be extended for longer than six months.'

'That's quite a list you've got.'

She nodded as she slid her hands up around his neck. 'It is. But I have someone to help me. Someone who showed me who he really was, showed me what mattered to him, before I got blindsided by my prejudices. I just needed the space to realise that. Well, that, and a cuddle from a very particular dog.'

'You went to the bookshop?'

She whispered in his ear. 'I don't know if you realise this, but Annie might be your number one fan.'

'She is?' He grinned at her.

'Oh, she definitely is. But then, she has good taste. Who can blame her?'

Avery hesitated. 'This might be hard. I might need to lean on you. The Paz family can be tough to face.'

'They don't know you yet,' she said encouragingly. 'They don't know what you have inside. Your clinical expertise, your knowledge of systems, your philanthropic nature, or how big your heart is.'

'And are you willing to be by my side?'

'Try and stop me.'

He bent and kissed her. 'I love you,' he said.

'I love you too.' She kissed him back, then straightened up and looked over her shoulder. 'Now, go get 'em.'

EPILOGUE

'WHAT TIME IS IT?' Robyn asked, anxiously sweeping things into drawers.

'Relax.' Avery smiled, his large presence filling the smaller part of their original cottage. 'They're not due to land at Edinburgh airport for another few hours.'

Robyn looked around. 'Do you think they'll like the place?'

Avery put his hand around his wife's shoulders and turned to face the back half of the cottage. The wide windows opened out onto a glen, complete with a running stream, gentle slopes, sheep and goats. Their extension and renovation had taken around six months and there were still little things to finish. 'How could anyone not like this place?' he answered simply.

Robyn sighed and put her head on her husband's shoulder. 'I'm just worried they'll think we should have stayed in San Diego.'

Serena, Toby, and their two-year-old daughter, Faith, were coming to stay for the next fortnight. They'd never been to Scotland and were anxious to spend time with their friends.

After a lot of soul-searching, and once Robyn had completed her programme, they'd both decided to leave San Diego. Avery still had his place on the hospital board, where he kept a very close eye on a much more subdued Leo, and, like many people nowadays, attended the meetings by connecting virtually. The soup kitchen and free clinic were still functioning, and Avery had even bought The Book Emporium after Annie had sadly passed away after a short illness, and installed new staff to run it.

Peggy, however, had come to Scotland with them. Both were working at a hospital in Edinburgh, a twenty-minute drive away.

'I have something to show you.' Avery smiled.

'Oh, no.' Robyn wagged her finger. 'You're up to something. What is it?'

He lifted up his tablet and turned it around. 'I think it could be time to expand this family. Peggy needs a friend.'

Robyn let out a gasp and leaned forward, glancing at the tired-looking dog in a basket, with a host of little wriggling puppies at her belly. 'Are those red Labradors?'

He smiled. 'They are. And one of them can be ours.'

'Really?'

He nodded. 'You told me just after we met that this was your plan. A house, a dog.' He gave a laugh. 'And I didn't give you much of a say in the first dog. So, it's only fair that you get to pick the second.'

Robyn breathed in. She couldn't stop the broad smile on her face, or the feeling of her heart expanding in her chest. 'How old are they?'

'Five weeks right now. We can collect ours in another month. There's three girls and three boys. We can meet them before you decide which one you want.'

Robyn threw her hands around his neck. 'Sometimes I think I've got the best husband in the world.' She kissed him on the lips.

'Only sometimes?' He quirked one eyebrow at her.

She raised her own eyebrows and kissed him again. 'Well, that just depends on whether we come home with one puppy or two,' she teased.

'Persuade me,' he said, his eyes gleaming.

And so she did.

* * * * *

If you missed the previous story in the California Nurses duet, then check out

The Nurse's One-Night Baby
by Tina Beckett

If you enjoyed this story, check out these other great reads from Scarlet Wilson

Snowed In with the Surgeon
Neonatal Doc on Her Doorstep
The Night They Never Forgot

All available now!